MY FIRST CRUISE

...by Timmy Aged 49¾

GW00392042

For my Mum.

Without whom I wouldn't be here.

Without whom I wouldn't be the man I am today.

Without whom I wouldn't have written all those wretched 'Thank you' letters.

Thank you and, as the person who always encouraged me to tell you a story, enjoy the buffoonery.

INTRODUCTION

I never anticipated seven months previously, when I retired from the Police, that I would be writing the introduction to this book. What I did know was that we were going to have seven months off together as a couple, doing different things that would bring us into contact with a wide variety of people. And, having never had a social media profile, mainly owing to my role in the police, I was bullied into occupying a meteoroid of cyberspace so our family and friends could 'follow' us. And I started to enjoy writing up our exploits to amuse myself... And if you hate people who breach all the laws of good, wholesome British grammar and start their sentences with 'And' ...and use copious amounts of '...' ...this book is probably not for you.

It began with a Blog recording our walk from Lands End towards John O'Groats during July and August 2018. That led on to joining a couple of well know social media platforms to record what we pretentiously called our, 'African Volunteering Safari.' Six weeks of this was spent with a fantastic organisation called Mercy Ships (www.mercyships.org.uk) working as Housekeepers on their Hospital Ship in Guinea, West Africa.

As time went by, I began to realise people I didn't even know were reading my posts and finding my take on life on board mildly amusing. Some were openly challenging me to write a book.

An idea began to birth that our upcoming Cruise might provide a rich seam of material for this very purpose. The positive response I got from sending out what you are about to read on Day 1 to a few friends, progressed that idea. So, instead of reading the three books I took, I found myself writing the one you are about to read. In case it has any success, I will be giving at least 30% of the proceeds to Mercy Ships. Amazon take 30%. The British Government will probably take the remaining 40%.

So, if it doesn't make you laugh, sorry, there are no refunds. Just rest in the knowledge you have contributed to yet another pair of Prime Minister Theresa May's leopard print court shoes to kick the Old Bill with.

More importantly, you have contributed towards a life changing operation for someone in Africa.

DAY 1 – GETTING THERE

The alarm goes off for the first time for a while at 6am on a Friday morning in January. For a Flight Time of 1.20pm? Really?!

Well owing to 'communication issues' Mrs F apparently didn't receive the message that the flight was today... to get on the Cruise Ship tomorrow... and had therefore scheduled all her life support appointments for today... CHAOS!

This all started to unravel in a crescendo on New Year's Eve. Nail graft surgery moved to Wednesday morning, check. Eyebrow revival, tint and shape, moved to Thursday morning, check. Hair transplant? "Oh dear madam, we can't do anything before 8.30am on Friday morning..." ...but we NEED to be on the road to Heathrow by 9.41am at the latest, my dear...

Marriage, as some of you well know, is one BIG compromise. In this, and in a number of other scenarios of late, I was on the losing side of this 'compromise'... having booked the flights 10 months ago for a relaxed start to the day, I was greeting the muted sunless January dawn with my beloved at 6am... albeit, her eyebrows were looking swell.

Thankfully, Miss F the 1st stepped up. She kindly deposited Mrs F at the Hair Clinic at 8.11am. This allowed me the time to pack a few pairs of... socks... for a Cruise. I find it immensely helpful to pack under pressure. It sharpens one's decision making. Suddenly it is not important that the shirt tie combo is a match, just that you have packed a shirt and tie. Creases appear less of a pressing issue. Drug choices are also easier for traveling hypochondriacs: just smuggle the whole contents of one's medicine cabinet into your wife's fourth suitcase.

Remarkably, the stars aligned in a Pay and Display car park in the sleepy market town of Failsham. Admittedly these stars were not on the scale of the astronomical display for Jesus's arrival some 10 days previously, but in the Funn Family, for Mr and Mrs F to arrive in the same place at exactly 9.30am, is supernatural.

...and the Hair Surgeon had done well. The quote from said esteemed Coiffeur to an elderly customer was, "I'm really sorry, but we have had an emergency this morning..."

...and so to Thiefrow.

...and their technology. I hate it when technology goes wrong. The Christian veneer is penetrated in seconds. WHAT DO YOU MEAN I CAN'T PRINT MY BOARDING PASSES?! I'VE CHECKED IN ONLINE AND IT ISN'T WORKING. WHY IS THIS FAMILY OF FIVE IRRITATING AMERICANS IN FRONT OF ME HOLDING ME UP FROM SPEAKING TO THE EMPIRE AIRLINES CUSTOMER SERVICE LADY?! WHY ARE THEIR TWO SONS PART OF THAT TEENAGE SECT WHICH HAD HEADPHONES IMPLANTED AT BIRTH?! THEY HAVE JUST RESIGNED FROM SOCIETY. BURN THEM AT THE STAKE. WHY ARE THEY NOT RESPONDING WHEN BEING SHOUTED AT BY THEIR PARENTS?! BECAUSE THEY ARE CURRENTLY IN *#@£)/ MUSICAL NIVANA. Lucky blighters. It has got to be better than the Empire Airlines Customer Disservice Queue.

More divine intervention. In frustration I look away from the Trump family and see some more EA staff slumped on desks doing nothing. Mrs F is despatched to interrupt Christine and Sharon's chin wag about the current price of Prosecco, to see if they can assist us. Mrs F turns, gives the thumbs up and the Christian veneer is resealed once again.

Just Airport Security to clear.

You know it is going to be traumatic when as you approach the Queue Management Fuhrer, she pulls the whizzy seat belt queue strap thingy across the apparently empty queue in front of you and directs you to one which appears to head into the horizon. And you wait. And wait. And when you can finally see the Security Search Area you realise why you are waiting: the Baggage X-ray Operative is having a nervous breakdown. It is instantly obvious that he is making that age old mistake of taking his job too seriously. His skin is white and clammy. His fingers are tapping restlessly on the armrest of his overworked swing chair. He is pushing his hand into his face and sweeping it across it repeatedly.

Up he gets again, throwing the swing chair behind him, to challenge an 83 year old disabled white woman about the 216 millilitres of stale Buxton spring water she has got in the bottom of her Sholley.

Steve needs to consider the wise words of an ex-Head of Sussex Police Criminal Investigation Department, Detective Chief Superintendent Samuel Fox: "You have got more chance of a golden eagle dropping a fridge on your head, than being a victim of a terrorist attack."

As part of his journey on the road to peace, Steve would do well to visit his Baggage X-ray Operative colleagues in Guinea. Fourteen days previously I had witnessed their 'work' first hand en route back from serving with Mercy Ships. It might just have been because it was midnight, but one woman seemed to manage the role single handedly whilst watching Desperate Housewives on a screen some distance from the X-ray equipment...

Gradually we got closer to Steve. It is ironic that the person most in need of a holiday in the whole of Terminal 6, was watching everyone else go on holiday. In an act of Christian kindness, I left him my brochure for Cerebral Cruises and blew him a kiss goodbye...

DAY 2 – ABU DHABI, UAE 6PM DEPARTURE

So, what's it like to board your first Cruise?

Well, like everything in life it depends on your attitude towards it. I used to get unnecessarily stressed about these things, but I have slowly learnt that where there are fellow Muppets, there is entertainment... and if you are not being entertained by them, you can be quite sure some Muppet will be getting their entertainment from looking at you... just look in the mirror...

The entertainment begins for us in a desert oasis called Abu Dhabi. It is what Hergé the Belgian cartoonist, revered author of Tintin, called 'The Land Of Black Gold,' one of the best books ever drawn. No fear of any Shakespearian quotes here.

The movers and Shiekers of Abu Dhabi have proactively converted its Black Gold into Concrete. Lots of it. Lashings of it. Tonnes and tons of it are being sprayed in all directions on a daily basis. They have had their most fun spraying it upwards and some of the edifices they have created are pretty impressive. However, if you stand still for too long in Abu Dhabi you end up with a concrete spray tan. Worse still, if you resist them in any way, you are issued with a free set of concrete boots and get to spend the rest of your life in Abu Dhabi, in the foundations of yet another hotel...

...but the best thing they did with their concrete was build a race track. We stayed the night overlooking this glorious spectacle and went to pay homage prior to finding our floating sun raft. It is of course one of twenty one Mecca's for Formula 1 aficionados and therefore obligatory to bow down and worship (Whilst Jesus is not looking).

The clear link you will have seen here is that one of the constituents of Black Gold is the fuel of Petrol Heads... and when that petrol is mixed with oxygen and you set fire to it, it EXPLODES! How can you not get excited by that? The noise of those continuous explosions within an internal combustion engine reverberates through one's soul in the same way that, I am lead to believe, a Class A drug courses through the veins of an addict.

Initially the Yas Marina Circuit was eerily quiet. We walked confidently through the doors of the five-star hotel that overlooks the circuit. Confidence gets you into most places in life. In this scenario, my confidence was boosted by a rather fetching Formula 1 Snapback (Keep up, it's a hat that looks even worse on a 50 year old buffoon than a baseball cap) with a Mercedes triple star on the front and the Union Flag emblazoned on the underside of the impossibly long peak. Five Star Class.

Thankfully, having taken the obligatory photos for the 'gram,' as we exited the hotel the silence was broken by the guttural roar of an unharnessed V12 engine. Who needs heroin?

...and so to the cruise terminal. Via a few sights in a taxi driven by Sean. The fact that 'Sean' was from Nepal didn't quite add up. However, he navigated us around the concrete without incident and cemented my belief I wouldn't be heading back to Abu Dhabi. With the possible exception of attending a Grand Prix.

I had never heard of Cerebral Cruises before we started these shenanigans. It sounded promising as it is not the kind of name that appeals to an Alpha Male. Omega Males maybe. However, they offered something no other cruise company appeared to be doing in our time frame, day trips to India. For precious white souls, India is a threat. Firstly, all Intelligence suggests that your personal space WILL be invaded. Having been invaded, secondly, your nasal canal WILL be assaulted. Thirdly, if you consume anything you WILL be terminated.

This is a constant uphill struggle for the Indian Tourist Board. However, as Mrs F has watched Bride and Prejudice, the desire to see the ground Mr Kohli walks on overrides all these threats.

As in his words, "No life without wife," mitigation was key to minimising these threats: take a ship to Kohliland with supplies; explore the carnage with fellow whities; retreat to the ship before dark. Dr Livingston would be proud of us.

So as Sean edged us towards Abu Dhabi cruise terminal at Mina Sayed Port, the anticipation began to build. It was not difficult to identify the Cerebral Cruises 'Erudite' as it was the only cruise liner in the concrete jungle. As we arrived at the taxi rank outside the terminal we were met by a tsunami of wonderful staff, all eager to please, smile... and take our money. They work for the great Mr/Mrs/Ms Cerebral and He/She/They employ 875 of them on board.

As Cruise Virgins, it was quickly evident that we were already off the pace. Check in opened online three days before departure. Every time I tried to log on to the Cerebral Cruises website, I got that helpful pop up: 'Sorry, there appears to have been a glitch.' This happens whenever I approach technology, so much so, that in IT squares I am known as The Glitch. I gave up. Turn up and see what happens I thought.

The time to arrive on the Erudite was 11.30am onwards... but it didn't leave the galaxy until 6pm. It later became clear that the majority of Cruisers turned up at 11ish, but as the queues were so long, an unimpressed Canadian tractor driver later told us that he didn't get onto the ship until 3pm.

We arrived at 3pm, handed our bags to some bloke who was hanging around outside the port, and headed into the cruise terminal. The first hurdle was security. They were not as interested in my snazzy Snapback as I would have liked. The second hurdle, rather bizarrely, was a photocopier. As we approached the 'Welcome to Cerebral Cruises' desk, I steeled myself for some teeth sucking judgement for not checking in.

Without introduction, the gentleman behind the desk said a little curtly, "Have you got your photocopies?" From nowhere I found myself saying, "No, I'm sorry we haven't checked in, your IT is rubbish." One all. Fortunately, things settled down into a more adult to adult interaction and we submitted our passports for ingestion by the Abu Dhabi Secret Police's photocopier.

Hurdle three was a marvellous example of that glorious phrase 'The first shall be last and the last shall be first.'

Ahead of us was a huge departures hall. On the right running the whole length of it were check in desks staffed by concrete workers on their day off. In front of them were queuing systems that would rival any international airport… and at various stages along them in order of Cruiser hierarchy were signs denoting where you should queue.

Royal Class. Presidential Class. Cerebral Class. Captain's Class… and so on. No prizes for guessing were we were. No Class. "Right at the end of the hall… Sir."

As we walked along, it became clear that all the Noble Classes queues were overflowing… but as we walked through the empty No Class aisles, the grin began to grow on my face. We walked right to the front of the queue and straight onto a check in desk. One-nil to the Cruise Virgins.

Check in only became interesting because of the clown checking in next to us. Santiago was lording it up over the poor old concrete worker at every opportunity. Mr Concrete 7639871 was the model of Customer Service excellence. Ten minutes in and Mr C had been left in no doubt by Santiago of his place in the food chain. Santiago clearly regarded himself as a major player in the Cruise fraternity and let it be known to all around him that he had been 'invited' onto this Cruise as a High Roller in the Casino. This was the smallest Cruise Liner he had ever deigned to grace with his presence. After twelve minutes of bullying, Mr C turned the tables having been told countless times by Santiago it was his birthday. With a flourish, Mr C stood up and rallied those around him in an international version of Happy Birthday. Santiago was visibly shocked that something so puerile could be happening to him... and, more shockingly, that no-one knew his name.

Onto our first Cruise Ship photo. Mr and Mrs Funn with a picture of the Cerebral Cruises 'Erudite' on a canvas background... Fraudulent. $100 off if you buy a copy in the first 3 days... Daylight robbery.

No Classers then had to walk to the Erudite, whilst the Nobility passed by in their blinged up golf buggies.

I used my limited human rights in Abu Dhabi to take a free photo of Mr and Mrs Funn with the REAL ship.

As we approached a line of Cerebral Cruises Gazebos leading up to the gangway, we were confronted with our first difficult cruising decision: iced water; iced water infused with orange or iced water infused with lemon?

I went with lemon to psyche myself up to board the ship. Then, taking great care to avoid the red carpet reserved for the Noble Classes, I strode purposefully up the gangplank.

It became clear that the majority of the other 2144 passengers were already on board and were working the 875 crew very hard. One member of crew for every two and half Cruisers. The ratio really translates as Crew 1: Cruisers 2, as it rapidly became apparent that the 'half' is just to account for the extra weight an average cruising couple are carrying.

Entry onto Deck 2 of the Erudite means that the first thing that greets you is the Medical Facility... followed by countless trays of champagne. Juxtaposition. I wanted to call my old English teacher, Mr Thickett, and thank him that as a result of his teaching, I could impress my readers by saying this was the epitome of juxtaposition.

It was difficult to find anyone not drinking champagne to accelerate their arrival weight gain. Experienced Cruisers clearly knew how to exploit these little fluted glasses as they loitered in the lift foyer. I saw at least two Cruisers go up in the lift, glass in hand, only to return down the stairs minutes later, minus glass... and pick up another glass of bubbles... back in the lift and cruise round again for another... They added a whole new meaning to the word 'cruising.'

As a statement of upper-middle aged independence, we took the stairs to our Stateroom on the seventh floor. Each lobby on the way up was littered with empty champers glasses. We worked our way valiantly round them, down the eternal corridor to our 13 square metres (140 square feet) of hutch space for the next two weeks. Calling it a hutch might be a little disingenuous, but the wire netting at the end gave us a good view of Abu Dhabi's finest concrete monoliths.

After the usual nesting routines, we decided it would be a good idea to 'weigh in' on Day 1 of Le Cruise, to set the bar. We did not anticipate that Cruising would become a sequel to the program 'Supersize Me,' but I rapidly began to change my mind. Using our learning on Mercy Ships, we made our way to the Medical Facility, as that was the place most likely to have an accurate electronic set of weighing scales to establish our initial Cruiser-weight. I suppose it was because we were still within the first few hours of free welcome champagne that the Medical Facility was empty.

Eventually, we attracted the attention of a dull Aussie who was wearing an awful lot of golden spaghetti on her epaulettes for a medical receptionist. It was clear Shelia had never been asked whether a Cruiser could weigh themselves voluntarily before. She was visibly rocked by the question. I contemplated delivering the haymaker blow - "Are there any dietary plans available?" However, Golden Spaghetti had already failed her sense of humour assessment, so I held back from an early knock down.

In the light of her surprise, it was no surprise that the Medical Facility could not offer weighing facilities. Golden Spaghetti recommended that we used the weighing scales in the Gym on Deck 10. In a generous attempt to allow her the opportunity to raise her sense of humour rating from zero, I asked her jokingly, "So, are they 'kind' scales, how do you rate their accuracy?" Complete blank. I booked her into her own Medical Facility for a Sense Of Humour transplant, and left.

Having weighed in, what does one do next?

Start eating of course.

On a cruise liner eating comes with a myriad of decisions. As it was our first night, we decided to try the 'Share a table with six other people you have never met before option' or 'Table Roulette.' Depending on who you end up sitting next to, it is very similar to Russian Roulette only, as I was to discover over the next few days, instead of being one bullet in the Revolver, there are six...

DAY 3 – DUBAI, UAE

The day begins by opening the curtains to find we have docked in Dubai. The view from the balcony starts in the foreground with a long snaking line of cream and rhubarb coloured Taxis. Mid-ground is occupied by the QE2. Remember her? The majestic Trans-Atlantic Cruise Liner has had an enginerectomy, been fully restored and is now a fully functioning Moby Carvery in Dubai docks. In the background, rising from the morning mist like an eternal line of skittles, is the stunning Dubai skyline. The tallest building in the world, the 828 metres (2,717 feet) tall Burj Khalifa, is the kingpin.

We spend a wonderful day in Dubai with our old neighbour from London. However, the day started to get a little pressured when petrol was required to return us to the ship in time. In Dubai, someone kindly fills the tank for you... unless it is change-over time when they don't... and we found ourselves wondering whether they really do leave people behind if you are late back to the floating rest home. Thankfully we made it into the 'Last Cruisers To Return To The Ship Top 10'... at numbers 11 and 10...

As we meander into the bowels of the ship, Captain Stavros commences his welcome back address over the tannoy system. Captain Stavros has the kind of Greek accent that makes you think his hands are reaching down from the speakers on the Ship and caressing ladies... ears. It is almost obscene. He moves serenely through the mundane process of welcoming people back on board the ship as we wind our way back up the midship staircase. As his announcement progresses, it is Manuka honey-glazed in its delivery... and from nowhere he delivers this line like a sword into the heart of every woman on board (Please read it in the euphonious tones of a Greek god):

"Remember life is beautiful, enjoy every moment of it."

Mrs F and various other ladies swooned on the midship stairs. Some men appeared to take advantage of the situation and reached out to catch women who were clearly not their wives. Absolute carnage. I have learnt from experience that ignoring your own wife and rescuing someone else's damsel, is like writing yourself a prescription for suppositories to be taken 16 times a day for the next 6 weeks. Two women cartwheeled past me as I reached out to catch Mrs F and execute a fireman's lift to deposit her in the safety of our 'Stateroom.'

Captain Stavros was there to. His seductive tones spilled out from the cabin tannoy and continued to hypnotise Mrs F. Eventually he bid everyone a very good afternoon and the spell was broken.

I made my way to the Bridge to politely remind Captain Stavros that he is employed purely to drive my ship.

You may be familiar with the term 'Mystery Cruises'. I had always thought the concept was that you turned up at a port and steamed off onto the horizon, stopping at ports you had no idea you were going to stop at, many of which you probably wish you had not stopped at all.

However, I have discovered 'Mystery Cruises' are actually happening all the time for the older generation. Take Stuart for example, who I met leaning against the handrail on Deck 11 as the ship departed Dubai:
"We went on a cruise round Great Britain last year... can't remember the name of the cruise company... can't remember the

name of the first port we stopped in... can't remember their name, but it was the islands off the top of Scotland... can't remember, but we then went to the islands off the top left of Scotland... can't remember its name but it wasn't actually Cork, it was the last port the Titanic docked in, posters telling you about it everywhere... can't remember how you spell the name of the port, but it has a 'g' and an 'h' in it... can't remember its name but it was a lovely little port in France... can't remember how many Cruises we have actually been on... oh I mustn't forget, it's my wife's 70th birthday tomorrow."

"Oh really, that's nice. Can you remember her name?"

As Cruise Virgins having your evening meal on a ship comes with a variety of questions requiring decisions. The first question is of course, "Do I want to eat?" Well, unless you have Norovirus, for Cruisers, the answer to that question is always, "YES"... and for 95 % of us it is followed by, "and LOTS of it please." As a consequence, with all their Cruising experience, most of the people on Erudite have steamed well past Cruiserweight, rowed themselves beyond Heavyweight and are sailing towards Deadweight...

So, what is an acceptable Cruiserweight? Well in this glorious world of diversity, this is of course an individual's choice. But do we have an opinion on it? OF COURSE WE DO! We all pretend we love the fat bloke with rolls of flesh hanging out the back of his grey towelling Adidas trackie bottoms as he leans over the balcony rail on Deck 11... but, if we were allowed to be honest, it actually repulses us. The majority of us deploy the 'look away' coping mechanism. Some of us however, cannot hide the reaction in our faces as he bends over the handrail and the loose adipose tissue shimmers in the noonday sun. Some of us are proactively watching out for those people's faces and obtaining free dopamine hits from the not so internal laughter that follows.

Your right, none of this helps define an acceptable Cruiser-weight.

Table Roulette took a new spin tonight.

It began with a debate over the difference a word makes. The waitress asks the question:
"Would you like a table for two or share?"

I thought she has asked:
"Would you like a table for two to share?"

Having established that foolishly we are going to attempt to bring some Funn into six people's lives, we head towards the Roulette Tables...

Tonight we are first to land and await with interest to see what Bullets 1 to 6 are going to turn out like.

It starts badly.

Bullet 1 is dea... f ♂
Bullet 2 answers for him ♀
Bullet 3 used to work for British Gas and clearly filled himself up with too much before he left ♂
Bullet 4 was having a night off ♀
Bullet 5 is the Silver Bullet and goes by the name of Selwyn ♂
Bullet 6 is a Psychiatrist who now has a full clinic ♀

Fortunately, we had a head start on B6 as we met her on the plane into Abu Dhabi. She is a seasoned Cruiser from America who works in difficult communities treating mental health issues. The debate therefore, is whether she is actually on Cerebral Cruises payroll... and why is she 'randomly' sitting next to me?

My fears were allayed within seconds of Selwyn sitting down on the other side of her. Selwyn's opening line to B6, having tucked his napkin into his open shirt, was, "Are you single?"

I nearly stabbed myself with my breadstick.

B6 handled herself like the consummate professional she clearly is. She gave Selwyn a short tour of her life whilst he was busy trying to attract the attention of the wine waiter. It was very clear Selwyn had already got good value out of his drinks package during the day.... but as he was aware there was plenty more red vino in the hold, Selwyn was intent on finishing it before we reached Muscat. In his best Welsh accent Selwyn greeted the wine waiter like he had known him all his life... which he probably had: "I'll have a luvely large glass of your best Pinot Noir, Monsieur, siv oh platee."

Once he had settled nicely into Glass 7 of the day, Selwyn began to engage with a conversation about the various nationalities represented on the ship. This conversation was further informed by B3 who was releasing gas at quite a rate about it. Apparently, there were 840 Brits on board, followed by 300 Canadians, meaning the Americans took Bronze. The general consensus on the table was that this 'win' was simply due to those of us trying to escape the cold weather in January. Selwyn managed to bring the conversation back to the fact he came from that English cul-de-sac called Wales.

B6 injected some intellect into the conversation by opening up a topic on Indian history... which led us on to the impact of the British... and as an American, her ancestry in England.

Selwyn had excluded himself from this conversation by ordering Glass 8. From nowhere he said, "I'm more British than Prince Charles."

Well that's one way of buying your way back into the conversation Selwyn, why's that then?

"Well he's half Greek isn't he?"

Fair point Selwyn, fair point. Selwyn explained to B6 that Prince

Charles father, Prince Philip was born in Greece, but, whilst we were cruising, was currently crashing cars around Norfolk. If you are familiar with that storyline, it fits in well with one of Prince Philip's best quotes:

"When a man opens a car door for his wife, it's either a new car or a new wife."

Or, in the case of Prince Charles, both.

Or, in the case of Selwyn, neither.

So Selwyn, where do you want to take the conversation next? ... No idea.

Table Roulette was looking more and more of an unstable game to play. Not only verbally, but physically. The Erudite was now heading towards The Strait of Hormuz, at the right hand end of the Arabian / Persian Gulf (Delete according to which side of the Gulf you are on). Anyone who tries to tell you that you won't be able to feel a cruise liner moving through the water is being more economical with the truth than this book. Even with a minimal White Horse count and no alcohol, Mrs F has been struggling to stay upright along the Ship corridors. Several Stateroom owners had opened their doors thinking someone was knocking, when it was just Mrs F's earrings swaying too far left and right and banging heavily against their doors. So, when playing Table Roulette, it is no surprise that you have to check the tide times in your glass before deciding when to take a sip. Selwyn's napkin had already changed from white to rosé and was on its way to having more Pinot Noir on it than in his glass...

Mrs F was desperate for attention next to me after enduring twenty minutes of B2 banging on about her experiences on Q & P Cruises. Whilst I was conducting the mental equivalent of CPR, I was aware that things had gone quiet between Selwyn and B6. B6 seemed to be finding a huge amount of interest in her napkin. Whilst I am not particularly good at listening to two conversations at once, it was difficult not to hear how Selwyn broke the silence. From nowhere he said, "What's it's like to have no history?"

I glanced across to see B6's reaction. She could clearly not believe what she had heard and in time honoured fashion, to buy herself time, replied, "Sorry what did you say?"

"What's it's like to have no history?"

B6 just stared at him in disbelief. After a few seconds Selwyn clearly couldn't cope with the silence and blurted out, "You know, you Americans don't have any history..."

Selwyn was not helping the 'Special Relationship' ...and he was clearly still going to be single when he left the table.

B6 struggled on towards dessert before she got hit with Selwyn's next Pub Quiz question:

"What are you going to do about Don?"

B6 had to buy some more time for this one. Having finally made the connection between Don and Donald, she summoned the last of her reserves from the bottom of her wine glass and strung together a brief synopsis of her views on President Trumpy for Selwyn to reflect on over Glass 9.

It transpired that B3 and B4 were in fact Selwyn's Carers, Samson and Delilah. They finally acknowledged their responsibilities as they got up to escort him to the 7.30pm Evening Entertainment Show in the Cerebral Theatre, leaving B6 slumped in her chair along with ourselves, the victims of another game of Table Roulette...

So, what was the Entertainment going to be tonight?

Last night we had made it to a spectacular acrobatic show at 7.30pm. It left Mrs F asking me why I couldn't hold her up on my feet whilst swinging from a rope 5 metres off the ground (Trying to appeal to a younger audience there, that's just over 16 feet). Owing to Selwyn's antics, we attended the second showing in the Cerebral Theatre at 9.30pm.

The nightly entertainment was introduced by Simon the on-board Cruise Director. That is a BIG title isn't it? It appears the Cruise Director Job Description insists you have to be an 'upbeat visionary.' A 'take-charge' person, who has a clear vision of how things should be. They will have a strong desire to be liked and for things to be pleasant...

Simon is also one of those strange breed of men who think it is acceptable to wear brown shoes with blue suits. He flounced his way onto the stage in his questionable beige brogues. For a man of such sartorial persuasion, coupled with the handicap of a Canadian-American accent, he did a half reasonable job of bigging it up for William. William was introduced as a singer with a particularly versatile voice. What does that actually mean Simon? No time to find out...

Great white spotlights began scanning intrusively across the stage like sharks circling a wounded whale... Mood music on a level well beyond that heard in the Asda foyer boomed round the auditorium... and suddenly it becomes apparent why the front section of the stage was missing. From the depths of the operatic pit, like a phoenix from the ashes, rises William... singing, at the top of his Welsh voice:
"I'm coming out, so you better get this party started..."

It was immediately clear that little Willy had actually come out a long time ago... as the only left-handed male in the pit village. The party was therefore in its final throws. Will had moved well beyond blue suits and brown shoes, to wearing a glitter infested black suit and silver sequinned studded shoes.

After his coming out song, Will gave us a little insight into his history, a synopsis of his play list for the evening and ended it with the line:
"Hopefully you are in for a treat."

It had already been a treat and after 'a little bit of pop'... and, "Well ladies and gentlemen we are going to visit a little bit of an Operatic period of time..." ...followed by the line, "You can talk to me I'm not the Pope," I felt well and truly treated.

The low point was when he threatened to sing something from Les Miserables. The very thought makes me feel thoroughly miserable. When I heard that my mate Ray has been to see it 18 times, I couldn't bring myself to speak to him for a month. And then they made it into a film. Russell Crowe should have had his equity card removed from him for life for appearing in it. From Gladiator to Les Mis: next step, gender reassignment.

Will ended with a well-rehearsed appeal:
"The way it works is this, this is my last song... but if you whoop and cheer enough I might just have another one in the bag.
Whilst I get to travel the world, I don't get to travel home very often. Well next week after six months away I am traveling home to South Wales. I will get to see my mother... which she seems quite excited by... and she will ask me...
Well, did you enjoy it?
And I will say, yes mother, I enjoyed it.
And did your audiences enjoy it?
[Muted applause]
Ohh, you are so kind, yes mother, they enjoyed it.
Did they whoop and clap and cheer?
[Muffled appreciation]
Two of them did.
Did they rise at the end of the last song with a standing ovation?
[Obliging titters in the stalls]
So at the end of this song, not for me but for my mother..."

Well, Just William went out to the strains of Cerebral Cruises Theme Tune, 'The Impossible Dream' ...and the journey he took 'To reach the unreachable star,' was emotional.

The audience were sobbing.

DAY 4 – MUSCAT, OMAN

Day 4 continues, according to Captain Stavros, at 17 Knots towards Oman. What use is that information to anyone on this Ship, Stavey?

Reader translation. For those aged between 0 and 35 years or our friends on the wrong side of the English Channel - 32 km/h: 36 to eternity, 20 mph.

Ask yourself what you know about Oman?

That is probably as much as I knew. One of my new Shipmates, Samson, thought it was in India. The Omani Tourist Board clearly has some work to do. Firstly, they need a new strap line. The current one is:
BEAUTY IS A PLACE

Umm, where shall I start. Firstly, that is a very bold claim when putting yourself up against the rest of the world. Secondly, 'beauty' is the wrong tense; a place is 'beautiful.' I always think the Queen has a very difficult job protecting her English. Thirdly, the capital Muscat doesn't help their case... starting with the Mus Cats that meet you at the entrance to the port: for goodness sake give the poor animals something to eat.

As you are probably beginning to realise, in my humble view, Oman is far from purrrfect. Dare I say it, they need the feminine touch. Put a Lady in charge for a while and add a 'W' in front of Oman, I say. In fact, I know the ideal candidate: our Mother Theresa will be out of a job shortly...

What is amazing about Muscat is entering the port on a massimo cruise liner. One of my preconceptions about Muscat was that it would be flat and sandy with a few tents. Well it is precipitous and rocky with a few lean-tos ...and that made it interesting, but I would stop short of using the word, 'beautiful.'

What was not at all interesting was Shawn from Birmingham in my left ear as we were standing on Deck 12 admiring the view. He latched on to a comment I made for the benefit of Mrs F about Captain Stavros earning his corn whilst navigating the ship into the harbour.

Before I irritate you with how Shawn irritated me, a few words on Topics.

1. The Number 1 Topic of conversation on the ship so far is of course... <u>Cruising</u>.

Cruising dominants the majority of people's lives on the ship and they want to talk about nothing else. Within seconds of meeting them they will have told you how many Cruises they have been on. When they find out you are a Cruise Virgin, you are bombarded with their Cruise Curriculum Vitae (CCV). They parade it around in front of you. It is like being back in the school playground - grown adults prancing up and down shaking their hips with their tongues out saying, "I've done 46 Cruises NERR NERR NA NERR NER!"

The most outrageous claim we had was someone who claims to have been on between 200 and 300 Cruises. I can't actually work out what they are proud of. They have paid to come on holiday on a ship several times. Why do they think that I think that is interesting? Why do they think I should be impressed by that? It is mystifying. They appear to be seeking admiration.

And then there are the Stats:
"So there are these two mega Cruise Ships owned by Royal Caribbean - one is TWO INCHES longer than the other and I have the choice. Well you know what happened, I found myself on it saying, 'Look, I'm on the biggest frigging Cruise Ship in the world!'"

So we were already heartily sick of people talking about Cruising whilst Cruising. We were also beginning to realise that there were very few fellow Cruise Virgins on the Ship.

2. The Number 2 Topic of conversation on the Ship is <u>Medical Problems</u>.

Beam me up.

If you were a Medical Twitcher, this is the place to be. Within minutes of being on this Floating Nursing Home you would have so many ticks against aliments that your pen would have run out. We have sat for our meals on tables of eight where our fellow diners have out sparred each other on their aliments.

You may be familiar with the experience when you tell someone you have been to Tenerife... and before you have finished sharing your best holiday story, they're telling you they have been to Elevenerife. Well having heard a lady tell the story of how she had had a devastating heart attack whilst on board a cruise last year, the bloke opposite her is out heart attacking her. I couldn't believe the insensitivity of it. He is banging on about what happened when his ticker stopped and I am starting to think unchristian thoughts... about wishing his heart attack had been terminal.

3. The Number 3 Topic of conversation on the Ship is <u>Drinks Packages</u>.

What this subject highlights for the benefit of Cruise Virgins out there, and particularly those who are now going to remain Cruise Virgins, is that on a Cruise Liner you are caught like rats in a trap / like shooting fish in a barrel / like lambs to the slaughter / like sardines in a tin / like taking candy from a baby (Please select the simile that best works for you).

As you will recall from Maslow's hierarchy of needs, one of the key physiological needs for a human being to stay alive, the foundation of the hierarchy, is water. There are some on the ship who would argue that Maslow's hierarchy needs updating –

there is now something more important than a human's physiological need for water: WiFi. We will visit that hypothesis later.

Water is therefore a great way of holding you to ransom when you are on a floating platform in the middle of a sea you have never heard of. If you think about it, as the Cruise Industry clearly has done, the drinking fluid spectrum begins with water and rises in value to the fluid worth, in some cases, even more than Black Gold, alcohol. Whatever you want to drink in the middle of the Arabian Sea, Cerebral Cruises is going to charge you a premium for staying alive. If you are somewhere on the journey to being an alcoholic, this makes you a rich seam of income.

So, just as there is a drinking fluid spectrum, there is a 'Drinks Package' that can be tailored for your needs... on a rising price spectrum: it will make your eyes water - so much so, you will feel like you will need to collect those tears and drink them, by the time you get to the top end of the spectrum...

If you enjoy predicting outcomes because it stops you falling asleep whilst reading a book like this, please fix in your head what you would pay in US Dollars for:

1. A one litre bottle of Evian water in your cabin.

2. Marinating yourself with (Almost) whatever drink you like on the Ship... in US Dollars... per person... per DAY.

At the time of typing, we are pre Brexit (If it happens. Brestay?) and you get 0.76 UK Pounds for the US Dollar... or, if you prefer, 0.51 Omani Rial's.

So, brace yourselves.

A one litre bottle of Evian drinking water: $5.50 (£4.17)

A premium drinks package: Starting from $69 per DAY (£52.32).

So, one of the many unanswered questions from this is, if $69 is the starting price, how much could I pay if I wanted certain specific drinks?

What does that mean in simple terms if you have a Drinks Package? It means you drink as much as you can. Wannabe alcoholics are hard at it from 6am onwards, pushing their trolleys along the bar... and falling off those trolleys by noon... 'troll-eyed.'

It makes for very interesting viewing when you are stone cold sober drinking two hydrogen atoms combined, by the good Lord Himself, with an oxygen one. All slightly ironic when you think that the same Lord combined one oxygen with one hydrogen atom to make the hydroxy group - alcohols. So the essential difference between one end of the drinking fluid spectrum and the other is one less hydrogen atom.

Where does all this leave Shawn?

Shawn is still as irritating as ever and he decided to talk to us about the Number 2 Topic of conversation on the ship - Medical Problems.

There is only one thing worse than talking about your own medical problems: talking about someone else's medical problems.

[Please read in a Brummie accent]

"... my wife had a knee replacement recently so we chose to come on this cruise. A few years ago she had the other knee done and we learnt a few things from that... but the key thing is that it all depends on the experience of the surgeon. ... so, for instance, if they have only done ten knee replacement operations then you might get some problems. ...whilst we can't say for certain, my wife had a number of problems after the first operation which could have been caused by lack of experience of the surgeon - you see what I mean. ...so when it came to the second operation..."

Suddenly Oman looked like a very beautiful place.

DAY 5 – AT SEA

A 'Day at sea'... A 'Day relaxing at sea'... A 'Day in the middle of the Arabian Sea wondering what this Cruising malarkey is all about'...

Well let me tell you it is not all bad! The biggest stress in the morning was finding Mrs F a table outside in the Sunrise Bar for breakfast.

This particular dining option means helping yourself. The Buffet is immense. It stretches on two sides for half the length of the Ship. Both sides are laid out the same: Buffet, gangway, troughs, windows. Diners lumber between trough and Buffet and back again with plates piled high with delicious cuisine from all around the world. The biggest risk to your health in this part of the ship is getting in between a Diner and the Buffet. Mrs F inadvertently made this mistake. She was waiting in a queue of two people for the blueberries when, from nowhere, an American lady appears from her left and delves into the bowl. Mrs F puts the polite challenge in:
"Are you in a rush or something?"
Mrs Kardashian:
"Well if you're not going to go, I'm going to go."
Mrs F was left speechless.

Owing to this kind of behaviour, we decided to refer to this dining option as the Food Zoo.

No need to go to the theatre for entertainment, just sit down and watch your fellow Homo sapiens at the 24/7 Cerebral Buffet.

This is where the Cruiserweights are piling on the pounds. It's happening, live, in front of you. Calories are being consumed on a gargantuan scale.

...and then it's your turn.

It is the choice that floors you initially ...and this is just for breakfast... Greek, American, English, Continental... well that helpfully reduced the choice by one... "Fresh omelette, choice of fillings, Sir?" "Belgium waffles with honey this morning?" "Pancakes dripping with maple syrup and a blob of cream?" I have made easier decisions when investigating murders.

As I couldn't find the Special K, I started with prunes.

Not.

An hour or so later as the live entertainment began to ebb away, Mrs F decided it was time to promenade on Deck 11.

Deck 11 has an oval path marked out on it in red as a walking track. Six laps is the equivalent of one kilometre (5/8 of a mile). On each side of the walking track are the ubiquitous sun loungers. Owing to the lack of Germans on the Ship, you have half a chance of getting one... and they are packed out this morning. Sun loungers for me have many similarities with mortuary slabs and, as the residents show few vital signs as we walk along, Deck 11 is referred to as The Mortuary Deck. Amongst the dead this morning is Sid who we met playing Table Roulette last night.

Sid is the reason why Mr and Mrs F have played their last game of Table For 8 Roulette. We arrived at the table first last night and took up position. After a few minutes a dark shadow crossed the table from five o'clock behind me and I glanced back to my right. What filled my vision, to the exclusion of everything else, was one of the most enormous bellys I have ever seen. Perched on top of it was a head which introduced itself as Sid.

What happened next is heavily disputed by Sid. Ordinarily one does not pay much attention to a man sitting down at a table. But this was no ordinary man. This was a man eight months pregnant with quadruplets. A hungry man, who couldn't wait to sit down.

Have you ever felt sorry for a chair?

I appreciate that feeling sorry for any inanimate object might be regarded as sentimental, but an awful lot of was about to be asked of this chair. For the rest of my days I will never forget the sight of Sid's knees bending in slow motion and the combined weight of five souls impacting the chair. Three legs took the strain. The left front nearest me partially failed. For a moment I thought I was going to be enveloped by this ball of tissue heading towards me. Fortunately, a combination of Sid's left knee and the Ship rolling to Port meant Sid was able to hold the position and gradually stand up accompanied by a torrent of expletives.

Sid is clearly not a man used to accepting responsibility: it was never going to be his 'fault'. Instantly he said, "The chair WAS broken!" A BIG commotion follows and a very disgruntled Sid moves to sit down on the other side of his wife. Any ordinary man would have negotiated with the Waiter and swopped chairs with an unused one on a neighbouring table. We are therefore left in a situation where Bullet Chambers 3 and 6 are left empty... meaning that no fourth couple can reasonably join us. This plays out over a couple of delightfully painful minutes. Eventually, Sid's wife Nancy volunteers to move. Sid creates an even bigger commotion about the fact it should be him and not her who moves back to sit next to me. Again a shadow crosses the table as he rises slowly to his feet, the quadruplets kicking out violently as he does so. The BIG question round the table now was, 'Will the new chair break?'

Sid shuffles towards his new victim. He positions himself, like an Olympic Diver on the edge of the high board, and the whole restaurant breathes in. Down he goes... and the chair... holds. It would be an exaggeration to suggest the chair received a ripple of applause, but in my head it did.

There was then the awful realisation that I was going to have to spend the next two hours listening to Sid talking through his thoughts on Topics 1 to 3.

...and that is exactly what happened. In that order. No more Table For 8 Roulette for me.

...and here was Sid on the Mortuary Deck, flat out on a sunlounger, belly well and truly up.

Call The Midwife.

No, hold on. Now that Sid's body was exposed, slavered in Australian Gold sunscreen, all became clear. We keep being told that, we are here, in the cradle of Buddhist thought - could it be that, right here in front of me, was the reincarnation of BIG B himself? What should I do first? Build a Temple? Rename the Ship? Call Sky News?

Mrs F told me, in no uncertain terms, to get a grip of myself.

The holiday accessory that has completely passed the Funn's by is the Sunlounger Towel Peg. These appear to be purchased as a pair and are affixed to the top edge of the sunlounger, trapping ones towel and preventing it from blowing away. They have ancillary benefits. Firstly they mark ones territory. In the same way that a dog lifts it leg and sprays a lamppost, a Sunlounger Towel Peg sends a clear message: Piddle off, this is MY sunlounger. Secondly, it allows an opportunity to express ones personality. Sunlounger Towel Pegs come in a range of whacky designs: flamingos, parrots, soldiers, Nemo...

...and if you are really part of the Sunlounger Set, you also have the Sunlounger Towel Strap. This natty little item wraps round the lower end of the mortuary slab and traps the towel against it. Personalisation is mushrooming and the printed strap line of 'Gone to the bar' really singles one out as a Funngi...

As we continue on our morning rounds of the Ship, I spy Selwyn and his Carers lying flat out in the Mortuary position. Mr Funngi goes straight in with the highly irritating opener of, "Morning campers!"
Selwyn nearly fell off his sunlounger. He would have done had it not been for the fact he was wrapped up like a Mummy in a number of Cerebral Cruises towels. As he was still half asleep, I took advantage:
"Look, he's got himself well and truly covered up - no chance of a suntan doing that Selwyn."
Selwyn was not only half asleep, he had had one too many Piña Coladas the night before. On account of the Cerebral Cruises hat he was wearing, I put in another body blow:
"And look at the baseball cap - you've gone all corporate Selwyn."
Selwyn came to life as I had just inadvertently pressed the money button.
"Ahh, there's a story behind that. I've got 15 of these at home. All lined up nicely in a cupboard... Yerr, I had to pay $20 for this one."

Moaning and gnashing of teeth followed. We learned a little more of Selwyn's story and how, "My beloved left me." This was clearly still a raw nerve. An equally raw nerve was the size of his cabin: "It's a broom cupboard. They have installed full length mirrors all the way down one side to double its size."

By now Selwyn's Carer's were well and truly getting on board and the conversation / bullying continued.

Never underestimate a fellow human being.

My world was about to be blown apart. I just didn't see it coming. I was in holiday mode enjoying a little casual banter

with new found friends. The sun was shining. Mr and Mrs Funn were standing on the Mortuary Deck with corpses all around us. Corpses with hearing aids. Having been disturbingly silent for a while, from nowhere, like a bout of Tourette's, Selwyn shouts out:
"YOU'RE A POLICEMAN!"

I was physically rocked by the power in that punch.

"YOU ARE AREN'T YOU?!"

It was as if Selwyn had pepper sprayed me. I was disoriented, confused, annoyed... so much so, Mrs Funn stepped in:
"Shhh... keep your voice down."
Selwyn: "So you are, aren't you?!"
Mr Funn: "I used to be. How did you know?"

I had not been outed like this for years. I took as much pride in not being recognised as a Cop, as being one. After seven months of detoxing from an organisation I had spent thirty years in, I was not expecting to have to provide my usual range of 'cover stories.' We Brits love to hang our identity on what we do for a living. Look out for it when you next speak with a stranger. I guarantee that, if they manage to stop talking about themselves, within two minutes they will have asked the question, "So, what do you do for a living?" I have spent thirty years dodging that question. Why? Because I am absolutely sick and tired about hearing YOUR story about why YOU were stopped by the ecilop!

That was wasted on Mrs F as well. police backwards. It's the first thing you see in YOUR rear-view mirror when you hear the siren / two tones / Nerr Nerrs (Trying to appeal to an international, cross generational readership) behind you.

I'm off duty for goodness sake. I last stopped a car when I was in uniform in the last millennium. I am not interested in the three points you got for driving at 37 in a 30mph zone. I have my own problems. On behalf of Police Officers Internationally, if you meet one who is stupid enough to admit they are one, please don't tell them your best police story. Within their number, there are some of the Funniest people on the planet, so if you frame your question carefully, you never know what they might tell you...

Cover story? If I really wanted to stop that line in conversation, in response to, "So, what do you do for a living?" ... in a slow, drawn out monotone: "I work for the Local Authority..." usually kills off even the most perky of interrogators. If I'm feeling more playful, it might be: "I'm in Security." This tests the enquirer's ability to ask the 'second' question... and gives a good indication whether they want to talk about me... or themselves. Sadly, 90% of people simply aren't interested or want to talk about themselves. Test that hypothesis for / on yourself. If I am in company, I will sometimes deliver the line: "I'm a part time Rabbi." This sets a Sense Of Humour baseline. As of seven months ago, things have changed: "I am retired." It is amazing how many people glaze over and are perfectly happy with that response... and the conversation moves on...

Selwyn wasn't happy.

Neither was I.

And the Mortuary Deck suddenly came alive.

Apparent zombies were rolling over on their slabs and wrestling to switch on their hearing aids.

Selwyn: "Well, you have an air of authority about you. I just knew you were a Cop."

There it is then. Select Self-protective Strategy Number 2: Change the conversation.

I succeeded in achieving this for a while and a few minutes of calm conversation ensued... but I was rattled and reviewing subconsciously, all the reasons why Selwyn might have known my previous occupation.

Selwyn had another bout of Tourette's:
"HAVE YOU EVER BEEN TO NEW ZEALAND?!"

Where was he going now?!

Mr F: "Well yes Selwyn, I have. Have you?"
Selwyn: "I have. I just wondered because I saw your belt."

Selwyn had benefited from a gust of wind that had displaced my shirt. It revealed my belt buckle which has a Kiwi on it and the words, 'New Zealand.' This Welsh pensioner was on it. I had to get away from him, lick my wounds and regroup.

You might recall that on our initial tour of the Ship we had visited the Gym to weigh ourselves. We had also looked at the obligatory Gym Classes... and looked away again as the average cost of a class was £20. Scandalous. Remarkably, people were still signing up. But I couldn't see Sid's name.

What did catch my eye however was a 'Life Enrichment Seminar: Solution to a Flatter Stomach.'

What is the difference between a Fatter and a Flatter Stomach?

'L'

What is 'L'?

'L' is a place...

... where the Devil reigns... but in this context, 'L' on earth is the Gym. Fatter to Flatter. No pain, no gain.

This 'Life Enrichment Seminar' was 'free.' ...nothing is free... so it will be a sales pitch... What for? Well, it's free and it's on a Sea Day, so I signed up... and rocked up at 11am.

At the end of the Life Enrichment Seminar there was indeed a sales pitch. This is your opportunity to commit to a price, in

dollars:
1. For a test.
2. For the cost of a product per month.
3. ... and how many people signed up for the test out of 15 attendees.

The first thing that was obvious on assessing the initial 8 attendees was that those who needed to be at this seminar were still gorging in the Food Zoo. So at one end of Deck 10 you had the 8 Lightweights + 1 in the Gym about to listen to a chat about flattening their stomachs. At the other end of Deck 10, in the Food Zoo, you had the other 2137 Cruiserweights and beyond, filling their faces to fatten their stomachs.

The Seminar was to take place in that empty space which you can visualise in most gyms. Whilst there is nothing there, if you make the mistake of allowing yourself to come under the 'control' of another alleged human being, it can be the most painful. It is the area in which 'Circuit Classes' take place ...and 'Zumba,' 'Steps,' 'Hit,' 'Cardio.' All titles that translate as pain.

Why do these areas of a gym always have a ridiculous amount of mirrors in them?

I am very aware of my physical shortcomings. I do not need to be reminded that, whilst I am enduring pain, I have a particularly BIG nose. Or to be encouraged to think about why the woman next to me has particularly BIG... ears.

#banmirrorsingyms

Today in this 'space,' collapsible chairs have been set up around a flip chart. Hovering around them was a hyperactive looking man who was as far from being a Cruiserweight as you can imagine. He was in the disgustingly good shape you would expect from someone prepared to present a seminar on flatter stomachs.

A few more attendees arrived and at precisely 11am this man came to life, introducing himself as Sergio from Slovakia (SFS).

It was immediately evident that SFS spoke very good English with staccato intonation. It is said that the average Cruiser speaks at somewhere between 125 and 150 words per minute: Sergio started at about 300 words per minute and maintained that pace for precisely an hour, no breaks, no meaningful audience participation ...but he did look lovely.

In the one minute SFS had allowed himself for his own introduction, the most significant thing he said was, "I was in the Slovakian army." Well he certainly had the 'guns' to suggest this was the case. In the nebulous world of Advanced Suspect Interviewing, Dr Eric Sheppard would have insisted on a whole topic area around this phrase. The Doctor calls it, 'Chasing vagueness.' The vagueness in this case is, 'What exactly do you mean by saying you were in the Slovakian army?' The parameters range from flipping eggs in the Slovakian Army Catering Corps, to committing war crimes in Special Forces, Slovakia (SFS). It was quite clear SFS wanted his audience to believe the latter.

SFS quickly settled into his rhythm:
"If you don't stick to a plan you will quickly lose your motivation. I am here to give you motivation. Do you want to me to be nice or to be honest? What is the difference between someone from Canada and someone from the USA? The difference is the latter is a little fatter..."

SFS was starting to cast his spell on a blonde lady on the front row. He asked:
"How many glasses of water should you be drinking a day?"

Before anyone could answer, she reached down to pick up her water bottle...

"What is your goal for today? If you don't have a goal, you will give up. You have to have a goal in your head."

A torrent of advice followed, summarised as: exercise more; stay active; eat less; die.

"How many of you have tried that before?"

"What?! Dying?!" said the woman next to me.

"No, die ting."

Chortles around the room. SFS's accent was excused on the basis his English is slightly better than my Slovakian.

No mention of the secret to making my stomach flatter yet.

Another ten minutes spent on everything from Body Mass Index to Basal Metabolic Rate. I was bored. Always a good time to have a sneaky look round to see how bored everyone else is. A glance to my left at eight o'clock reveals that Stanley is already asleep. His bifocals are in danger of sliding off his nose. At seventy, he is still waiting to receive the memo that explains it is unacceptable, in 2019, to pull your white socks up to your knees.

Others behind me stir from their slumber as I crane my neck round in search of further amusement.

SFS crashes on undeterred. The first word that starts to sign post the sales pitch is 'nutrition.' The first phrase that starts to make it clearer: "We need to reinvest. Invest in organic chicken."

A little anecdote follows about Mary which, condensed, plays as: Mary came to one of my seminars, but would rather spend $3000 on a diamond necklace, than 513 organic chickens.

I like Mary. She actually walked out of the seminar before it finished. Respect. None of us were going to be brave enough to do that now, were we? Might get a knock on the Stateroom Door at 3am from Special Forces, Slovakia...

What difference was eating 513 organic chickens going to make to a 79 year old woman anyway?

SFS then led us on a little dance through toxins, medication, drinking, acids, coffee, sodas... Stanley was now at forty five degrees in his chair, heading towards horizontal. I spent a few moments wondering whether he had signed a 'Do Not Resuscitate' form before coming on the Cruise...

Back in the room, SFS was now highlighting the horrors of an additive called aspartame. He was getting so passionate about it, I was thinking I should wake Stanley up.

SFS spoke authoritatively about the fact that aspartame is possibly related to health effects ranging from mild problems such as headache, dizziness, digestive symptoms, and changes in mood, to more serious health issues such as Alzheimer disease, birth defects, diabetes, Gulf War syndrome, attention deficit disorders, Parkinson disease, lupus... Oh, and you might find it in Cola drinks...

SFS was particularly anti-Cola. A rant ensued. How much sugar in every teaspoon of Cola? Two teaspoons ...apparently... How much aspartame? Gallons of it... apparently. It's really, really, really, really toxic ...apparently.

I don't think I was the only one in room wondering where on earth SFS was heading, as you probably are right now...

He continued on a fresh rant about cortisol v adrenaline and finally said the word stomach:
"Show me the size of your stomach."
Suddenly SFS had my attention. The way he asked it was as if he was issuing an order in the Slovakian Army. I honestly thought the blonde lady on the front row might stand up and expose herself. Stan was obviously dreaming about that happening to, because he nearly gave himself whiplash waking up. Fortunately, clarification was sort before she could stand up and SFS explained he meant the size of the actual stomach organ, as opposed to the average Cruiserweights stomach, as in belly / paunch / food baby.

We were finally getting to what SFS was trying to sell us.
"You can get the necessary alkalines to reduce the acid levels from things like spinach, asparagus, broccoli... but one of the

reasons the Japanese are so healthy is because they get theirs from various seaweeds and algae's in things like Sushi..."

SFS was then making the connection between the damage toxins do to the liver... time for the SCARY, you must therefore buy my product, video.

Cue: YouTube video, Dr Drew's Lifechangers: bad liver v good liver. Gruesome mortuary footage of respective livers. Cue: Lots of wincing and sucking of teeth in the audience. Stan adjusted his bifocals.

Followed by SFS's best line: "What is the best fat test? Take off all your clothes and shake your body."

Stan glanced hopefully at the blonde lady on the front row.

Here it comes after a 55 minute build up.
SFS: "...but I cannot do anything for you unless you take the test. I cannot do anything without the test results. The test is $67."

The audience is decidedly non plussed. Wasn't this seminar supposed to be about flatter stomachs?

"...and, subject to the results of the test the cleansing product I would be recommending costs $150 a month, that's 4 to 5 Dollars a day... for six months... if you want to take the test, please come and speak to me at the end."

Squad dismissed.

I hung around, pretending to sign up for gym classes, as my fellow potential Slovakian Army recruits filed despondently out of the gym. If you committed to no-one signing up for 'the test,' you were correct.

What does one do on a ship after a motivational seminar like this?

Rush back to your Stateroom, reach inside the fridge and pour yourself an ice cold Cola of course. It was delicious.

After enjoying it on our balcony overlooking a mirror glass smooth Arabian Sea, I did have a look at the Cola bottle. The great advantage of buying a 2.25 litre bottle of Cola in Dubai, to avoid the hideous prices Cerebral Cruises would have charged me, is the product information is in Arabic. No need to worry about the sugar or aspartame content here SFS. Just drink more of it...

[These are not the words of a responsible adult: the author is injecting 'pathos' into the abstract. Please make your own informed choices about Cola. Better still, read a decent book]

DAY 6 AND 7 – MUMBAI, INDIA

The tannoy in the corridor crackled into life at 6.30am and, as the Captain couldn't be bothered to get out of bed, Mrs Stavros the 3rd announced our arrival on the Indian subcontinent.

It never fails to amaze me how easy I am to irritate.

I should have been delighted to know that, having never thought I'd make it, I was in India. However, at 6.30am I was decidedly unimpressed. In this case it was all about timing. What time is it acceptable to use a tannoy? 8am? Ship Clubbers would have only just gone to bed so they might not agree, but if you had a Ship Referendum, I think 8am would be the earliest you could get Cruisers to agree to.

I was so unimpressed about being woken up, I couldn't get back to sleep. At 6.47am I decided to go out onto our balcony in one of those natty little white napkins they inform you is a dressing gown. As I opened the sliding door of my Cabin it was nasally clear we had arrived in India. No choice now but to man up and spend an hour soaking up last night's spices: Mrs F was not going to let me back in the Cabin without some strong, marriage threatening feedback. So one hour ahead of me in the dark... in a space measuring 9 by 4 feet (2.7 by 1.2 metres)... freezing cold... the air smelling like a rotting chicken madras... wearing a white napkin... with nothing to do... apart from curse Mrs Stavros. It left me reflecting on whether, when they trademarked 'Tannoy', they deliberately included the word 'annoy'?

Mumbai Harbour was pitch black and we were facing the sea, so initially there wasn't much to see. However, boats / ships / floating skips were moving around and a few of them belonged to the Indian Navy. As dawn broke I progressed through my routine Yoga stretches in an attempt to keep warm. This involved the usual Cat Pose (Marjaryasana), Chair Pose (Utkatasana), Cobra Pose (Bhujangasana), Conqueror Breath (Ujjayi Pranayama) and my favourite, the Corpse Pose (Shavasana), which goes down particularly well on the Mortuary Deck.

By the time I got to the Cobra Pose I realised that the amount of Indian Navy Patrol Launches passing by was increasing dramatically. It was dawning physically and metaphorically on me, that my white dressing gown was gathering a cult following in the Indian Navy. At least five different Indian Navy Patrol Launches were taking it in turns to pass, loiter and snigger at the insomniac Englishman in a napkin on Deck 7 doing unrecognisable things with his body. You could see the launches wobbling in the water with laughter. Realising I was causing a bit of a stir, against my introvert nature, I decided to play to the crowd. When all you are wearing is a napkin, there is not much else you can flaunt without getting arrested, but I fluffed up my Chest Wig and began to assume the Chair position with fresh vigour, placing my hands against the balcony handrail.

Having held it for 60 seconds, rising up, I lunged into the Warrior 3 (Virabhadrasana III) position. To those of you who have never invested time in understanding Yoga moves, this culminates with standing on one leg with your body, arms and other leg in a horizontal position, perpendicular to the standing leg. As I am so slim these days, everything was in line with the balcony handrail and all the Indian Sailor's would have seen through the glass below the rail was a single standing leg... Not buying it?

Well, the Indian Navy were loving it. I had a flotilla of Launches lined up watching as the sun rose majestically, piercing its way through the Mumbai morning mist. Mist would be charitable. In reality it was a dirty, acrid layer of air pollution that enveloped the city.

45

The problem with having so many Launches in a small area is that they create waves. Waves rock a Ship, however BIG it is. Men balancing on one leg on a balcony wearing napkins are unstable both physically and mentally... however hard I try and convince you otherwise, you will think I fell over. I maintain that, with a little divine assistance, I moved positions... from Warrior 3 to Corpse Pose... and I didn't knock myself out, I choose to stay in that position until the Indian Navy repositioned their fleet.

When I did eventually stand up it became clear now it was light that, as a piece of income generation, the Indian Navy had sold Cerebral Cruises a berth. All around us were Destroyers, Battlecruisers, Submarines and even an Aircraft Carrier. All I came for was a decent Indian Takeaway.

Owing to the early start, Mrs F declared we would trial a breakfast in the restaurant. To date, we had never made it there as they finished serving at 9am. Having settled into a window seat to enjoy further Indian Navy morning manoeuvres, we were joined by an unusual pairing on the table next to us, a fag paper away. Two men. One white, one Asian. One Jewish, one Indian. One 69, one 28. One wearing a flat cap, round mirror shades and white sneakers. One wearing a trendy T-shirt, shorts and flip flops. Saul and Sanjay.

Having settled in, Saul was the first to engage with us and quickly had us enthralled on various subjects which didn't include Topics 1 to 3. After a few minutes, Mrs F separately interrogated Sanjay, and I focused on Saul.

Most of what Saul said is unprintable. He was immensely entertaining, but was willing to fully exploit his right to freedom of speech. A little bit like this book, it was difficult to work out whether what Saul was saying was true, or whether he was saying it for effect. Non-fiction or fiction? Truth or lie?

I felt the need for a gentle challenge when Saul delivered the line, "When I used to go to my performances in London."

"When you say your performances, what do you mean?"

"Well, I was a member at Covent Garden for two years. I came across from New York to see Joan Sutherland. She was one of the great bel canto singers of the 20th century and performed at the Covent Garden Opera Company. The great thing about Concorde was you could leave New York in the morning and be in London by half three - we used to meet up in Upper Brook Street and then go and see Joan perform - oh, it was so special."

"How many times did you go on Concorde?"

"Oh, about ten - it was such an exclusive club - I spoke with all the greats - Jack Lemmon, yes, and Henry Kissinger - his wife Nancy, she was a right old thing, the Royal Family, oh yes, they all travelled on Concorde."

It made a pleasant change from talking about Cruising...

Time for our first experience of organised shore excursions. Mrs F was keen to be there at the allotted time of 9.15am in the Theatre. It was clear as we approached it that this was a big day for shore excursions. The Theatre was heaving with anxious Cruiserweights. Like us, it appeared the majority did not trust themselves with orientating their way around Mumbai. Owing to the Cerebral Cruises Indian Scary Story Department, most appeared to have bathed in antibacterial hand gel, donned facial masks and had sun hats with brims wider than the average cricket pitch. The atmosphere in the Theatre had the feel of an adult school trip about it. The Headmaster, a Mexican called Sebastián, had a very soothing voice over the Microphone trying to keep his anxious pupils calm. Seb issued a steady stream of directions and called out each trip by number. The fact we were 23 illustrates just how many had signed up.

Eventually 23 was called and we filed off the Ship, checking out with Security as we did so. In front of Mrs F was Scott Wright, 54, from Solihull, Birmingham and he had a Classic Drinks Package.

How do I know that? As you check in or out, all your details flash up on the screen for everyone around you to see. During the excursion, I 'sense of humour tested' Scott by using his name in the middle of an inane line about his wife delegating him responsibility for photography. He failed the test and was avoided for the rest of the Cruise.

The Indian Army Privates operating the Security X-ray machines could do with a briefing on Customer Service. Greeting tourists by cleaning their noses with the business end of an AK47 does not constitute a warm welcome to a country. The Indian Immigration Officers had evolved a little, they cleaned your nose with a pen.

At least with a clean nose you got the full benefits of Mumbai's free aromatherapy as you exited the Cruise Shed. The next challenge was fighting your way past numerous offers of a taxi, to Coach 23.

What happened next was made mildly more compelling by the fact we did a very similar tour the next day. This highlighted that the information you receive on a tour is entirely dependent on your tour guide. What follows is the comparison between the 'facts' you hear on Day 1 compared with the 'facts' you hear on Day 2. The 'facts' have been subsequently checked on Boogle. On both days our Tour Guides were female, but the only thing they had in common was bad breath.

The dabbawalas – a lunch box delivery system – facts not in dispute
It's a homemade lunch, delivered to office workers who can't go home to eat it. Also known as dabbas, the delivered lunches are transported in circular metal tins. Each dabba comes in between two and four tiers. The bottom one is the largest, with rice, while the others include a curry, a side of vegetables, flatbreads, a dessert and an Elizabeth Shaw mint. I can tell you from my ob-

servations at pavement level, that the percentage of these metal dabba's in use, compared with a modern insulated lunchbox, is low. The BIG unanswered question is why on earth can't these office workers carry their lunches to work themselves, like the rest of the world? This system also exposes the Blue and Pink jobs in Indian culture: all the indications are that the vast majority of the office workers are male, and the vast majority of those making the lunch, are female.

The key people in this delivery system are the dabbawalas – which translates as "one who carries a box." They wear a white kurta uniform which looks like a smock, crowned with the traditional Gandhi cap.

Day 1
1. Approximately 200,000 dabbas are moved each day by an estimated 5,000 dabbawalas.
CORRECT

2. Harvard Business School studied the dabbawalas process and graded it 'Six Sigma,' meaning they make fewer than 3.4 mistakes per million transactions.
CORRECT

3. Even Richard Branson has spent a day learning the dabbawalas' secrets.
CORRECT

4. A unique alphanumeric code is scrawled on each metal lunchbox which ensures it arrives at the right destination.
CORRECT

5. Dabbawalas earn between $12 and $15 per month.
INCORRECT $150 and $175

<u>Day 2</u>
1. In 1932, 3 British Army Officers devised the system to deliver their lunch.
INCORRECT In 1890 Mahadeo Havaji Bachche started a lunch delivery service with about a hundred men in Bombay, now Mumbai.

2. 0.00001% chance that Dabbawalas might make an error.
CORRECT

3. Between 22 to 26 lunch boxes are carried on a bicycle.
CORRECT

4. Monthly charges for the dabba service range from 1200 to 1800 Rupees per month, depending on the distance and time taken.
INCORRECT 600 to 1000 Rupees

5. In Indian culture there is an acknowledgement of the need to support service industries, so whilst it might be cheaper to buy food whilst at work, office workers sometimes choose to support the Dubbawalas.
CORRECT

3/5

1:0 to Tour Guide Day 1.

<u>Dhobi Ghat – an open air laundry – facts not in dispute</u>
The washers, known as dhobis, work in the open air to flog, scrub, dye and bleach clothes. They do this in concrete wash

pens, dry the items on ropes and neatly press them.

Day 1
1. Dhobi Ghat obtained a Guinness Book of World Records entry under 'most people hand-washing clothes at a single location' in 2011.
CORRECT

2. Their main business is cleaning clothes and linens from Mumbai's hotels and hospitals.
CORRECT

2/2

Day 2
1. At most times of the day, over 7000 dhobis can be seen working from the original stalls that date back to British rule.
CORRECT

2. The men do the washing; the women do the ironing.
CORRECT

2/2

Bonus point for Tour Guide Day 2: During a piece of commentary about the vagaries of getting married in India: "...my husband says that their facial expression shows whether they are married or not, no need for a certificate."

Tour Guide Day 1 **1**: Tour Guide Day 2 **1**

Draw. Fair result. Both asked to share the prize, a bottle of breath freshener.

Day 2's excursion ended in an astoundingly dull museum and we bailed out as soon as possible. We promptly bumped into some new Shipmates on the pavement outside who had inspired us to get back into Scrabble, the wonderfully frustrating word game. Scott and Bailey were a proper couple from up North who lived on the hard shoulder of the M1. They had a few twists on Blue and Pink jobs in a relationship. Scott earnt the money, Bailey spent it. Scott did the drinking, Bailey did the smoking. Scott had breakfast, Bailey didn't. Scott listened, Bailey spoke. Scott played Golf, Bailey told us all about it. They were lovely ...and, after a few more days, they let us play Scrabble with them.

Have I had a rant yet about the cost of the WiFi on the Ship? No? Well it's about time I did. It is yet another example of how the Cruise Industry alienates its Cruisers. Like it or not, access to the World Wide Web has become a necessary evil, even on holiday. Ask yourself what you would be prepared to pay per day for Internet access, bearing in mind that most people already have unfettered access as part of a contract. Let me start you at £10 per day. No, that won't be enough. £20? Not enough. £25? Are you still in? This gets you the basics... for one device...

This leads to some interesting effects on Cruisers. A fair proportion of them are more interested in Free WiFi than the port they have arrived in. A new breed of Tourist has arrived: the WiFi Explorer. Like WiFi ants leaving the Ship, they file off in search of local Free WiFi Hotspots. Fellow WiFiants follow them and pass WiFi Intelligence back along the chain. WiFi Explorers become almost as boring as Cruisers: "We did ever so well today, found a café in the Port that had great download speeds... spent five hours there in the end - didn't spend a penny." "See any of the city?" "No, not really bothered... seen it all before."

Well I had become a victim of this WiFi famine and had identified that Moonbucks, Mumbai were going to quench both my thirst for decent caffeine and WiFi in one glorious dopamine high. Finding Moonbucks was the problem... with no internet connection and only a fleeting glimpse of it on the coach trip the previous day, we were on our own in the Mumbai Jungle. Well I say that, as a man of faith, the good Lord was with us, just not sure whether He is that fussed about Moonbucks. So with me physically was my life partner, Mrs F, who regularly complements me on my sense of direction. However, she is willing to do what no real male can: ask someone for directions.

So, having been quite happy up until this point following me, she asks Scott where Moonbucks is. Why would Scott know? Scott asks Bailey. Why would Bailey know? Bailey asks the art vendor at the side of the road. He had never heard of Moonbucks. Bailey asks another poor unsuspecting Indian who also has never heard of Moonbucks. All because Mrs F does not trust her husband, four other people have lost precious minutes of their lives unnecessarily. Even if they did know, not all the streets in India have names... and, if they do, they do not all have signposts. What happened next, always happens. Scott started to make a case for it being 'that way' on the basis of no evidence whatsoever. This then creates conflict. I am going the opposite way, because I always was, before Mrs F decided to ask Scott.

Somehow, I now had to explain that, despite all this really helpful input, I would be going 'my way'... Having worked extremely hard to leave Scott and Bailey without losing the opportunity to play Scrabble against them in the future, I then had to justify myself to Mrs F. She made this as difficult as usual and made it very clear that I was now on my own and would be held to account if Moonbucks wasn't located... quickly.

Every now and then I astound even myself. After following my considerable nose, four streets and three junctions later we are ordering a Flat White with a WiFi code in... Costars.

Having sated our thirst for information and caffeine we headed back to the Ship. One of the first people I saw on board was Selwyn with his Carers. They had not left the Ship. It had not even occurred to me that some people might choose not to leave the Ship on Day 2 in the same Port. I never really understood his rationale for not leaving, but, as with everything in life, it was his choice and I had to respect it... and Selwyn didn't give a monkeys what I thought about it anyway.

The conversation moved on to Selwyn's late morning (9.15am) Gin and Tonic. Selwyn explained that having ordered his G&T, the Barman thought he was doing him a favour by tipping out the considerable remains of the bottle of gin into the glass. Selwyn summarised the effects of this with the line, "It has been a difficult day since." His Carers nodded rather too vigorously in agreement.

Time for an open question for Selwyn. Characters like this in life never disappoint when you set them up with an open question: "So, what was your favourite thing about Mumbai?"
Without a milliseconds hesitation Selwyn is back at me with: "The Laundry."
Drama queens never give you their rationale for an obscure answer, they leave a silence, waiting for you to ask. If you don't play their game and meet silence with silence, they sulk. They are looking for the echo:
"The Laundry?"
"Well I don't understand how they get it all back to the right people..." and so he continued...

As the Ship left Mumbai we watched from the aft end of Deck 10 in an outside bar. On the adjoining table were a couple in their 80's who visually raised the question, "Who on this Ship is on their last Cruise?" Apparently it is not unusual to 'lose' at least one Cruiser during a Cruise. We were already aware of a few 'medical emergencies' which were spoken of in hushed tones amongst fellow Cruisers. This couple had not weathered well, but to their absolute credit, they were not sitting in a nursing home somewhere on the south coast of England doing crosswords, they were doing those crosswords on a floating nursing home in Mumbai.

Mrs F is an expert in death. Without engaging with this couple at all, she diagnosed that the man had Chronic Obstructive Pulmonary Disease (COPD), was a long term smoker and this accounted for his poor circulation, swollen ankles, rampant skin psoriasis and poor mobility. Despite all this, he made it to the bar for a Jack Daniel's and Coke. Would it be his last Cruise? We will never know.

DAY 8 – GOA, INDIA

Another opportunity to have breakfast in the restaurant arose and we snatched it. A table by the window Sir? Oh yes please. And a fag paper between you and the next table? Well, it seems to be the thing.

Our neighbours this morning had actually been in front of us in the queue, but they had been faffing about so much it had actually got Mrs F's goat. It is not often complete strangers bring out the goat. Mrs F is one of the most tolerant people I know, so it is always more fun to see her goat trotting into view. The challenge is establishing the reason the goat was released. In this case the goat release clause was triggered by rudeness to staff, coupled with a failure to observe a simple queuing system.

The fact that they were a diminutive Korean couple in their eighties cut them no slack from Mrs F. By the time we got to the table, I was getting sprayed liberally with goat's milk. When they ended up next to us, Mrs F made the dangerous assumption that they didn't speak English: "You see, if they had just waited they would have had this table wouldn't they?" Time for an urgent change in conversation to slay the goat. Food choice is always good neutral territory for Mrs F. I even volunteered, whilst on holiday in this desperate set of circumstances, to eat some fruit to keep the goat out of sight.

We placed our order and settled into conversation about the forthcoming day.

At an unidentifiable break in our conversation, the Korean gentleman asked in perfect English:
"Excuse me, what language are you speaking?"

I was slightly bemused.

"English."

"Ah, my wife thought you were speaking German."

... and they both collapsed in laughter.

Being accused of speaking German is no laughing matter.

But it did mean they could laugh which was a currency Cruisers are not always blessed with.

Mrs F's goat quickly trotted over the bridge and these Koreans had her in their thrall in no time.

The conversation went on hold whilst they placed their order. Seth and Betty had been married 63 years, but that did not stop Betty getting some feedback about how much food she was ordering. Place the condemnation, with heavy intonation by Seth, on the first word:

"THAT many dishes?"

Betty held her nerve.

This played out ten minutes later with so many plates of food, they could barely fit them on the table. In the middle of one of them was a hearty slice of bright yellow frittata (An Italian take on a thick omelette or the British equivalent, fat quiche). Seth didn't hold back:

"That's HUMONGOUS."

This was made all the more amusing when Seth revealed he had been Professor of Politics at Pennsylvania University... and Betty had been his Librarian.

I decided it was time to check in with Betty:

"How is my German?"

Oh how she laughed.

Asian ladies put Mrs F to shame. They know how to laugh obligingly even when a man's 'joke' is not funny.

Imagine the tears of laughter she shed when it came to say goodbye and I wished her:

"Auf Wiedersehen!"

Fast forward 84 hours to a closing set of lift doors in the Forward

Lobby. Just as we see each other from ten metres away, Betty leans out of the lift, waves her right hand and says in a loud voice, "Auf Wiedersehen!"
What a woman.

Goa = Nice beaches. Author fell asleep.

DAY 9 – COCHIN, INDIA

Couldn't blame the Tannoy this time. I just woke up and realised from the change in engine speed that we were arriving in Cochin. Apparently, it's pronounced 'Ker-ching' as that is the sound you hear the locals make as a Cruiser when you approach any of the shops in the town, 'Kerching, Kerching!'

By the time I got onto the balcony we were in the Port and manoeuvring towards our berth. Dawn was just breaking at 6.25am and a long line of coaches were already in position. I breathed a sigh of relief as we were facing the Port side with no signs of the Indian Navy to admire my white napkin. Taking some learning from last time, I put my nice brown socks on...

As the light improved, the line of coaches continued to grow. If you want a coach in India you can have one in any colour you want, as long as it's white. However, in order to individualise their coaches, a few sign markings are often added. The one that caught my attention as it thundered into view had emblazoned along each side, 'Noah's Ark.' Interesting marketing. Are you implying your customers are animals? Even more bizarre in this context: a coach calling itself the Ark was coming to a huge Ark like Ship to pick up predominantly elderly couples, two by two, to take them on a tour and return them back a few hours later, so that they can sail off somewhere else: what on earth would poor old Noah think of all that?

The early start secured another sumptuous breakfast in the Restaurant. You might recall that only Scott does breakfast and we had the pleasure of sharing it with him. It was a great opportunity to learn a little more about him... and invite ourselves for a game of Scrabble. This prompted a 'trousers' moment. You may be familiar with the phrase 'Who wears the trousers' in a relationship. In our ever changing world, it is only a matter of time before the Politically Correct Language Police ban it. However, traditionally it helps indicate where the balance of power in a relationship sits and, in this scenario, Scott was a Loser. He did however agree to negotiate with Bailey about whether we could be allowed to play Scrabble with them, and would report back. Bailey's decision on our fate was clouded by the fact that whilst she was away from her Scrabble Board the previous day, Mrs F had tipped Scott a seven letter word which had ultimately won him the game...

We did our morning rounds of the Mortuary Deck looking for signs of life. First up for Morning Moaning were Sion and Sian. It was a light-hearted question, just checking in, making sure your OK, not really interested, but feel obliged, "What did you do yesterday then?"
"Well we had two hours in a coach looking at the untidy town of Goa." Before I could stem the flow, the tide of moaning, wailing and gnashing of teeth was heading right at me. What did she expect from a coach trip entitled, 'A Glimpse of Goa.'
"...and the coach had these odd curtains it did, which meant you couldn't see anything out of the windows... and after about 45 minutes of driving through dullness, we got to a market... BUT THEY ONLY LET US OUT OF THE COACH FOR TEN MINUTES! ... good job mind, all they had there was carrots. Lots of carrots. ... I just wanted to go shopping."

Should have stayed in Cardiff luv.

Our tour of Kerching actually started in the Cerebral Theatre with an inadvertent introduction to our fellow tourists. We didn't know it yet, but The Addams Family would be on board. And they were already causing a commotion in the lobby of the theatre.

If you are unfamiliar with the Addams Family, to have any chance of understanding what follows, you need to have a basic understanding of the Addams Family tree.

Gomez Addams is the patriarch of the Family, is married to Morticia and they are parents of daughter, Wednesday and sons Pugsley and Pubert Addams. Morticia has an Uncle Fester. Grandmama is Grandmama. Lurch is their 6 ft 9 in (2.05 m) tall, shambling, gloomy butler.

We arrive in the Theatre unwittingly following Wednesday who meets up with her parents Gomez and Morticia just in front of us. No warm welcome for Wednesday, Morticia starts with:
"Your late, you've made us late, why are you late?!"
Wednesday: "I'm not late, it said to be here at 9.45 and it is 9.44."
Morticia: "Why are you late?"
Wednesday: "I'm not late. I am here before the time."
Mortica: "We have been worried about you. Everyone has been waiting. Uncle Fester got here, why can't you?"
Wednesday: "Look, I'm here now, we can go."
Mortica: "Well we are waiting to be called. If you had been here on time we might have got a different number and be gone by now."

This was playing out at high volume to all of us waiting to be called to our respective Coaches. Gomez is silently loitering behind Morticia and we are yet to understand who the rest of the Addams Family is, amongst the throng of anxious Cruisers. Apart from Lurch of course, who is towering over everyone looking bored already. Having said that, there were quite a lot of tall, shambling, gloomy men on the ship, so never assume. At this point, we don't know that the Addams Family will join us on Coach 14, so this is just a wonderful family domestic argument playing out for our delectation. It is remarkable how, when another family are having a row, everyone around them goes silent and tunes in. Even Morticia became aware of this and after a few more snipes at Wednesday, she marched off to look at some apparently fascinating water bottles on a table nearby.

It wasn't long before Headmaster Seb's soothing tones were re-assuring us that all was fine and dandy and Coach 14 had been beautifully prepared for our wonderful excursion. Wonderful excursion? Well, this one was marketed by Cerebral Cruises as 'Kerching At A Gallop,' so a faster pace, amongst 'coconut covered islands and rich green forests,' over four hours was in prospect.

So, we filed out of the boat with the WiFiants, jostled our way through countless offers of a Tuc Tuc, to another white coach and took up our customary position on the back seat.

Now, as someone who believes we are all made in the image of a God who has blessed me with a considerable and ever extending, bright red proboscis, please read what follows in that context.

As I watched my fellow Homo sapiens joining me on the coach, for whatever reason, you could not have collected together a more motley set of human beings. There was enough work on this coach to keep a plastic surgeon in business for a lifetime. It was like an International Diversity Party minus any athletes. Youth to, was a poorly represented minority group, but as Wednesday dragged herself up the aisle as if it were Monday, it dawned on me that the Addams Family were coming on board. For those of you who have followed the cartoons and films over the years, you will realise, on appearance alone, it would usually be easy to identify Addams family members: however, they blended into this coach load of fellow extras in a horror movie, perfectly normally.

As Coach 14 began to fill up, two other Youth Reps got on board. Pugsley Addams was of course one of them, already with his head in a large packet of Jay's Crisps. No sign of baby Pubert Addams, he was probably having his moustache coiffured in the Ships Barbers. The other Youth was Ramona, a wisp of a 5 year old girl with long blond hair. Her thin stature was exacerbated by the colossal size of her parents. Whilst I don't know anything about their lifestyle in Paraguay, I do know that it involves a huge amount of eating. In fact, I suspect they are on the Cruise because they ate all the food in Paraguay.

Time to meet our Tour Guide, Siad. Siad begins with a, "Namaste," and then raises lollipop number 14 to welcome us into his temporary family. He had no idea what a hard days parenting lay ahead for him. As the coach rolled out of the port, he began to outline what a gallop through Kerching was going to look like. The coach was pitching and rolling in a similar way to the Erudite, and Siad was struggling to stay upright whilst talking into a 1950's microphone, as he tried, valiantly, to make Kerching sound interesting.

As I looked forward down the coach it was the typical scene you might expect on such an excursion. Apart from Morticia. Morticia immediately identified herself as 'odd.' She was sitting in Row 4 on the left, in theory in the aisle seat. Only she wasn't. She was actually sitting on Gomez's knee which meant from where I was sitting it looked like she was very uncomfortably placed on his left knee leaning forward through the middle of Row 3 to give Siad her full attention.

Siad's view was that of a 55 year old American woman peering intently at him whilst breathing heavily into the ears of those in Row 3. Her face looked like it had been caked in white stage make up, but it was of course Factor 67. The crowning glory was her hat. I will never have the insight into why Morticia found it necessary to wear a hat on an air conditioned coach. The hat could well have been homemade as its 'design' smacked of melanoma paranoia. If you imagine an iconic image of the planet Saturn with its resplendent rings, cut it in half horizontally, paint it nebulous beige and put it on Morticia's head, you are looking at her hat. The brim drooped over into Row 3 nudging the ears of the two passengers periodically.

It was just over two minutes into Siad's commentary that Morticia started interrupting him. Siad was selling Kerching on the basis of the weather: "It's 30 degrees centigrade. Every day. This is cold. This is winter." He exposed his pearly white teeth and paused for effect. Morticia was in:
"Have you heard of Basmati rice?"
A combination of yet another pot hole and that question, physically knocked Siad off balance. Siad's pearly whites disappeared and his face contorted into a look of disbelief:
"Yes madam, I have heard of Basmati rice."
Morticia: "We have Basmati rice in America. Does it grow here?"
Siad dug deep: "It does, it grows in the foothills of the Himalayas in northern India."
But the best was yet to come: "Some varieties actually grow in the US."
As a Tour Guide I am sure you are asked some difficult questions, but two minutes into a tour when talking about the weather and you get a question in the Agricultural Genre… and you knock it out of the park, respect.

Was Morticia impressed?

Of course not. "Yes, I was aware of that." Integrity alarm. Did Morticia know that? Would you have known Basmati rice can be grown in America? I am not saying she has been convicted of lying, but on the balance of probabilities, I feel it is unlikely she is an expert in the cultivation of Basmati rice.

Further questions followed from both Morticia and other potential Addams Family members. Poor Siad was struggling to manage his audience and this was all at variance with the Tour Guide script in his head that he had learnt that morning. It led to a very fractured delivery and the 'loop' he had rehearsed about Kerching International Airport moving locations we heard at least twice. It wasn't interesting the first time.

What was interesting were Siad's observations about crash helmets. These, to be fair, were more in evidence here, than on motorcycle riders in Mumbai:

"Dis is Mahatma Gandhi Road. Dere is Mahatma Gandhi Road din every town. As u can see the motorcyclists wear de crash helmit. But de passenger dus not wear de crash helmit. Dis is one of de advantages of being a Hindu. We believe din reincarnation. So if u die u have a chance to wear a crash helmit later." Pearly whites out. Pause for effect.

Now that we were aware of the Addams Family, the first tour stop focus was not on galloping off to the Temple, but on piecing together the Addams Family tree. Getting Horror Movie Extra's off a coach is a painful operation, especially when coupled with crossing a road with Hindu's busy trying to get reincarnated or put you up for reincarnation. However, if you earn your living as a Zombie Film Extra, you are in your element. Lurch lurched into the road on our behalf, like any good butler should, and his sheer presence brought everything to a halt. The motorists at the front of the queue then had the free entertainment of a freak show passing across in front of them. This was more and more like being in an Addams Family movie.

My confidence in Siad's credentials as a Tour Guide then took a knock. Lollipop 14 is initially bobbing along a fence line beside a road when suddenly it stops, works its way back through Tour Party 14 (TP14), through a gap in the fence and into an area of rough ground. We all re-orientated, Baaa like sheep and follow along. Initially all appears well as we are distracted by what should have been the wonderful sight of a bull elephant in the shade of a tree. However, the scene was clouded by the fact the elephant didn't appear overly happy and was chained up. That didn't stop TP14 from filling up a couple of terabytes worth of pixels to record the elephant for the benefit of anyone who wasn't there. It was so impressive, I think TP14 might have been able to hold their own in a Terabyte Challenge with a Japanese Coach Party. I didn't say win, I said 'hold their own.'

As I looked round I realised that TP16, which happened to include Selwyn and his Carers, was debussing behind Coach 14 and heading off in the opposite direction. Meanwhile Siad had approached a local man who happened to be wandering across the rough ground, and was asking him for directions. As a consequence Lollipop 14 continued across the rough ground for a hundred meters to what turned out to be the Temple wall. We then walked across the Temple rubbish tip, past an open fire in a cavernous hole and through another fence into a car park. Yes, the rubbish tip contained all the things you would expect to find in a rubbish tip.

What I was not ready for though, was a series of explosions coming from the Temple area. Involuntarily I ducked and turned instinctively towards the sound fearing for my life… but quickly realised by the complete lack of interest from the locals, that it was firecrackers set off to announce Selwyn's arrival at the Temple. He later told me that the walk from the Coach to the main entrance was fifty metres. I will spare you his description of the effects of a close quarter encounter with firecrackers on his sphincter muscles.

From the car park we ended up back on the road we started on in the first place and therefore could have walked along it without getting our shoes covered in recycled elephant food and been here ten minutes ago. Siad then took us on a circuitous route another four hundred metres to a Temple entrance via the obligatory stalls selling Tourist related detritus. This whole journey sent the Addams Family into free fall. We had begun to realise that the Addam's Family had expanded considerably since the last Film. In fact, we were starting to think we were the only people on Coach 14 who were not members of the Addams Family. Gomez was working particularly hard to keep the family spirits up. 'Kerching At A Gallop' had been advertised with cautionary advice: 'Note: This tour is not suitable for guests with limited mobility. Walk approx. 200 yards over flat, uneven surfaces.' No mention of a Temple rubbish tip and bonfire. And, whether you are working in yards or metres, you will have noticed we are well past 200 yards… and we have got to get back yet…

I hung back in TP14 which was now strung out across over one hundred metres behind Lollipop 14, to enjoy the chaos. Grandmama Addams was flagging and verbalising her discontent to Gomez. Her views on being walked through 'A Temple $|-|1+ hole' cannot be recorded. Three paces behind her is a grumbling Uncle Fester who wants to know whether he is going to be able to get yet another wonderful samosa at the Temple Takeaway. Pugsley Addams had finished his family pack of Jay's Crisps and, in the absence of a sun hat, had fashioned the foil Jay's Crisps bag over his head. The remaining crisp crumbs are scattered over his shoulders, creating the impression he has rampant dandruff. Wednesday had joined that Sect in which headphones are implanted at birth. Morticia was frantically moving between apparently, as yet, unidentified members of the Addams Family asking them to look out for Basmati rice.

What happened next was to become one of the highlights of this whole shenanigans. We continued to pick our way past the stalls into the main Temple area and gingerly found our way to a side entrance which gave access to the central area. This gave us a restricted view into the Temple forecourts from whence emanated the kind of backing music you will be familiar with in your local Indian restaurant, but at fifty times the volume. What it didn't prepare me for was the majestic sight of a bull elephant in full ceremonial regalia rounding the corner towards me. It was an awesome spectacle. The elephant had three men on top of it waving a variety of articles, the only language for which I can find is, pom-poms. This makes them sound like Elephant riding Cheerleaders which would be hugely disrespectful. Suffice to say, words cannot do justice to what I saw that day, as, one by one, seven Asian bull elephants came into view and lined up for the next part of the ceremony.

Here comes the 'but'. It has always been the same in everyday life, someone pays a compliment in order to buy themselves space to say what they really think and the pivot point in the sentence, between positive and negative, is, 'but'. Well here is the negative and calling someone a Numpty seems entirely appropriate when the complaint involves their inability to get you the best view of an elephant.

You will have picked up that Siad missed the main entrance to Temple and had to ask directions to get us in. Well I would have forgiven all that with good Christian grace, but what I really saw as a consequence of this lack of Tour Guide leadership, were seven Bull Elephants in a line mooning at me. Admittedly it was seven BIG moons. Whilst I have always secretly wanted to be part of a Mass Moon, I have never been brave enough to join one. Having surveyed the crowd of worshipping Hindu's, experience told me this was not the time to start. Something intuitively told me that a couple of shrivelled white English prunes bending over next to seven Asian elephants in a Temple might just have put my Indian Visa at risk.

However much you might love nature, the ass end of an elephant is never going to be as attractive as the trunk end. Particularly when the elephant has spent six hours in makeup. If this was the best view I was going to get as a white Caucasian Christian male in a Hindu Temple, I would have accepted that. But Selwyn, his Carers and the whole of ruddy Coach 16 had been correctly tour guided to the centre of the Temple forecourt and, worst of all, I could see them all revelling in the full frontal, trunk end view of seven Asian bull elephants. Every possible appendage of members of Coach 16 was clutching some form of pixel creating device recording this incredible sight from THE FRONT ROW. I was just a couple of inconvenient pixels in the background of their footage, tucked behind the fifth elephant's impressive family jewels.

Siad is a Numpty.

Having hung around for a while hanging over the Temple wall and managing to take a few snaps of Coach 16 taking even more snaps of the elephants, Siad declared it was time to leave. So we dutifully retraced our steps and watched as the Addam's Family tried to perform a roll call whilst exiting the Temple. Having declared the elephants to have been one of the highlights of the whole trip, following in a close second was the sight of Gomez in full flight chasing after Uncle Fester who was disappearing onto the horizon in search of further samosas.

Gomez appeared from behind me on my left, at full tilt, in a proper state of panic. He was wearing Size 14 unbranded white sneakers, white towelling socks pulled up to just below his knees, Bermuda style shorts and a whacky pink Hawaiian short sleeved shirt. Gomez was clearly not familiar with running. The synapses between his brain and his limbs had clearly been damaged at some point, as his legs and arms were so physically uncoordinated. You knew it would only take one rouge electrical nerve impulse to bring his 6 ft 6 in (1.98 m) frame crashing down onto Indian terra firma. It was mesmerising to watch and for a moment all work, chatter and movement in the area outside the Temple stopped to watch Gomez 'running' and shouting, "Uncle Fester, UNCLE FESTER, STOP!"

Uncle Fester was having none of it. He dodged right out of our view in his quest to find the best samosa in India, and into a maze of stalls. Shortly afterwards, and against all the odds, still upright, Gomez followed him. Along with Wednesday. Along with Pugsley. Along with Morticia. Siad was left looking after Grandmama. And the rest of us. TP14 came to halt as the Uncle Fester steeplechase continued. No one seemed to mind, this was live Addams Family Drama unfolding in front of our eyes. What was interesting in hindsight is that no one else, including ourselves, volunteered to help chase down Uncle Fester. It was almost as if non-Addams Family members on Coach 14 had already worked out, in the first hour of being with them, that this was 'normal.' Sure enough, after a couple of minutes Gomez, Uncle Fester and the rest of the family appeared out of the maze of stalls all talking at once and externally processing their part in catching Uncle Fester. Siad wisely set off before they joined us, towards the coach.

There are times on these tours when you realise your Tour Guide is struggling for points of local interest. When you are driven several miles to cross a bridge over a river to an island and then back again over the same bridge so 'you can get a view' over Kerching, you realise you won't be galloping back to it. Particularly when the bridge is no more than 10 metres above the river. The coach doesn't stop. There is nothing to see. I was left thinking I would not want to be reincarnated as a Tour Guide in Kerching with such ungrateful tourists.

We wound our way back from the spectacular viewpoint along exactly the same roads, past exactly the same shops with exactly the same commentary, in reverse. We passed the aerodrome and learned about Kerching International Airport moving locations, again. We then entered fresh territory, but the commentary remained the same, until we reached a "Women's Craft Cooperative Shop." Hide your wallets Gentlemen.

This was evidently shopping evolution in action. Many readers will have been subjected to that experience abroad when you are asked by a man what you want to buy and then you are hustled off down a side street to one of his 'cousins' to look at something completely different. Well, it became clear from Siad's commentary that Indian women had wised up to the fact that us foreigners were bored of this tactic, and they had developed a more subtle way of reducing Western bank balances.

This is the way it worked from a 'Customer experience' perspective. Coach 14 arrives in an apparently residential street and stops in the middle of it, helpfully preventing everyone else from going about their business. A cluster of sari wearing women scuttled out of a house and gathered around the coach door greeting the occupants of Coach 14 like members of the Royal Family. The Addams Family absolutely loved this attention and milked it for all it was worth, as they were escorted to what transpired to be a converted house packed full of... Female view: Glorious fripperies. Male view: Absolute tat. As I was becoming accustomed to elsewhere, the shopping assistants cleverly disguised in sari's, immediately tried to thrust upon you a natty little bright coloured plastic shopping basket. Hasn't emasculation gone far enough? I like to think my ego is not yet as big as The Shard, but asking a 6 ft 1 in (1.86 m) male with the hippest Ray-Bans in Kerching to carry a small, bright pink plastic shopping basket? I wrote this down straight away on my customer feedback form, in my best Urdu. Having refused the offer of one shopping basket, by the time I had been offered one for the eighth time, I was wishing I had a smaller ego.

The next tactic the "Women's Craft Cooperative Shop" deployed was drinks... followed by food. As you are aware, FOOD is a BIG Button for Cruisers. And it's free? OH YES!

Do you remember Ramona? She is the five year old on holiday with her gargantuan parents from Paraguay. They happen to be in the foyer of the shop with me (Closest to the door, in the hope of leaving) when the food starts coming round. In the meantime, I have tuned into some 'mixed messages' from Ramona's family. Bearing in mind they are from Paraguay, the first odd thing is that all these messages are displayed in English. Ramona herself has a sweet little pink T-shirt with some flouncy writing on it: "Radiate Positivity." Her father has a white cotton sheet wrapped around him with an emblem and the words:
"Bugo Hoss: In Green We Trust." Her mother has emblazoned on her mobile phone cover for all to see: "The BITCH is back." Lovely family.

One of the shopping assistants, cleverly disguised in a sari, approaches Ramona with a small basket of peanut cookies. The family leans in around the basket. A discussion follows about what they are and how delicious they look. Despite liberal encouragement from her parents, Ramona turns down this, once in a lifetime, offer. Needless to say, her parents took two each.

Morticia had totally immersed herself in this 'Shopping Experience.' She had her own Personal Shopper, cleverly disguised in a sari, who is being kept very busy following the top half of the planet Saturn around the shop – you never know where those ultra-violet rays get these days. The Personal Shopper is in turn shadowed by Gomez who is understandably looking nervous about his bank balance. To my delight, this little entourage arrives in the foyer. I had completely failed to observe that next to me, from floor to ceiling, was every spice India could squeeze out of its agricultural gross domestic products. It is this that Morticia focuses in on. There is nothing quite like live entertainment. I had been reminded of that by the excellent entertainment shows on the Erudite each evening. This however, was niche live entertainment, about to unfold next to me.

One of the advantages about being an ex-police manager is that I have been Surveillance Trained, albeit, at a Special Needs level. This means that, for instance, I was once allowed out of the Surveillance Vehicle I was in, to buy a coffee. By sheer coincidence the subjects we happened to be surveilling, decided they too preferred Costalot Coffee. To my horror, I ended up in front of them in the queue... and I was able to inform my Squad what their target was as a result of listening to their conversation. They never let me out of the vehicle again. In a "Women's Craft Cooperative Shop," in a foreign country, with no technical equipment and no extraction team, there are many aspects of Surveillance Tradecraft to consider. I worked through the checklist in my mind and considered my options carefully. In the end, I decided the best option was to: Remain standing still.

It is impossible to convey in writing the nuances of silence. Morticia was clearly giving her Personal Shopper the run around on the prices of spices, and deploying silence as a tactic to intimidate her into reducing those prices. Apparently, vanilla pods are very desirable. Until recently I thought vanilla simply meant 'white,' as in white ice cream. Yet another 'knowledge gap' my dear parents failed to fill. The Personal Shopper was working hard to update Morticia that, apparently, the price of one kilo of vanilla pods has gone up by over 500 per cent in the last few years. Gomez winced. Morticia was not impressed, so the Personal Shopper continued delivering fascinating facts about vanilla. Apparently, vanilla has been fetching upwards of $600 per kilo. What does that really mean Personal Shopper? It means vanilla is about $60 per kilo more than the price of precious silver. I never knew shopping could be so interesting.

As I was smiling at Gomez's pain, my own heart missed a beat as I was reminded that Mrs F was unsupervised in this emporium. Instinctively my right hand reached down to my shorts pocket to check I still had my wallet. Yes, I still had initial control. Just had to brace myself mentally for the 'approach.'

This negative thought took the gloss off the ongoing live entertainment next to me. Morticia was a skilled manipulator. She was placing spices I had never heard of into the lime green plastic shopping basket the Personal Shopper was carrying on her behalf. A few moments later, she would pick one up from the basket and put it back... almost... she would hold it there in front of its allotted position on the wall, wait for the Personal Shopper to announce a remarkable drop in price and then place it gently back in the basket. All this was done without Morticia saying anything. It was like silent poetry. The only person who wasn't enjoying it was Gomez. As the basket filled up with enough spices to keep all the Indian Restaurants in a small American State happy for a decade, Morticia ploughed on.

It was now the Personal Shoppers turn to use silence as a weapon. Somehow without making any obvious noise or movement, she communicated to a fellow sari wearing shopping temptress that another lime green plastic shopping basket was required. The transition was seamless. I have had the 'privilege' of watching South American handbag thieves operate at Heathrow with a level of criminal professionalism that, strangely enough, if it wasn't criminal, could be admired. That was the level the staff at the "Women's Craft Cooperative Shop" had been trained to. The empty lime green plastic shopping basket changed places with the full lime green plastic shopping basket and neither Morticia or Gomez even realised it had happened. As the full one disappeared towards the Checkout you could hear the silent "KERCHING!" ringing out on the faces of the sari wearing shopping temptresses behind the till.

How many other shopping baskets Morticia filled I do not know, as she suddenly realised there was an 'upstairs' to this shop and the entourage followed her childlike excitement up the stairs. Suffice to say, judging by the amount of bags that arrived back on Coach 14 and the additional lines on Gomez's face, it was several.

Remarkably, the 'approach' from Mrs F never came. She reported that she had tried on a very nice dress, but could not manage to negotiate a price which she regarded as reasonable. I am far too wooden to be an actor, but I did my best to feign disappointment.

Mrs F's position was at complete variance to the report we heard from B6 later about her visit to the 'Women's Craft Cooperative Shop.' B6 had been on a different excursion called, 'Kingly Kerching.' It became clearer and clearer upon speaking with her, that these excursion titles bore no connection with the tour you actually went on. They were all just an excuse to get you to the 'Women's Craft Cooperative Shop.' The more I think about it, all four words in the title press BIG Buttons in the female psyche. The gender word, 'Women's.' The arty word, 'Craft.' The community word, 'Cooperative.' The euphoric word, 'Shop.'

B6's experience was a similar tale of luminous yellow plastic shopping basket, Personal Shopper and peanut cookies. Whether there is something we might class as illegal in the peanut cookies is up for question as, from the point she nibbled her first one, B6's judgement began to erode. By her own admission, things that she would ordinarily say no to, suddenly seemed like a really good idea. Bearing in mind B6 is a Psychiatrist, this is even more worrying. What hooked her in were the spices. She had previously bought a well presented collection of mixed spices as gifts for friends back in the less United than they used to be States. The 'Women's Craft Cooperative Shop' had a wonderfully packaged array of locally produced, vegan friendly, no added preservatives, a percentage of the sale goes to the local orphanage, we'll press one of your buttons, spices. B6 is not sure she even has ten friends who might enjoy cooking with spices, but somehow, ten packages of mixed spices found their way into the luminous yellow plastic shopping basket.

B6's next 'button' is scarfs. What is it about women and scarfs? Are they simply jealous about men wearing ties? Both are essentially a noose in disguise: invert it, lift the person off the ground suddenly and they are dead. What are the Health and Safety Executive doing about this?

#bringbackelasticatedties

I used to work with a sane, well informed, intelligent woman called Marie who wore a scarf to work, every day of the year. Why did she need a scarf when it was 30 degrees centigrade? It was baffling. Could she help me understand the female fascination with scarfs? The best insight I got was, "I just like them." OK. I can live with that, but you are sweating all over my desk. You are familiar with pseudonyms - a fictitious name, pen name, assumed name, alias, false name, professional name, so-briquet, stage name. Pseudonyms are used in the shadowy world of intelligence to refer to targets without divulging who one is referring to, unless you know the Operation. Different agencies have different rules on pseudonyms, but it is generally accepted that it is two words, often an adjective and a noun. Why is this relevant? Marie's pseudonym was Permanent Scarf. When B6 admitted to being a Scarf Addict, she was unwittingly pressing one of my 'buttons.' What could I learn from her about this scarf addiction?

B6's eyes lit up when she found the scarfs, rows and rows of them. To the male eye this just looked like a pile of oily rags. To the female eye it is clearly something altogether different. Is it about colour? Texture? Patterns? Feel? All of them? My line when I was growing up was that I lived in a female dominated household: mum, two sisters and even the dog was a bitch. Has this insight into the female brain helped me understand their fascination with scarfs? Not in the slightest. Direct question to B6 about why she had such an unhealthy interest in scarfs? "I just like them." No further forward then. As long as there are women like B6 and Permanent Scarf on the planet, the Indian Scarf Industry is safe.

B6 placed seven scarfs in total, one for each day of the week, into her luminous yellow plastic shopping basket. She then attempted to work her way towards the checkout via various other items of interest, carefully presented to her by her Personal Shopper. When B6 relayed this tale to us, what she was most embarrassed about was what happened next. What happened next, fuels the belief there is something illegal in the peanut cookies. B6 maintains that usually she is very aware of how much something costs and whether she considers it reasonable value. She acknowledges with hindsight that she had no idea what any of the items she purchased cost or the exchange rate between the Indian Rupee and American Dollar. When she was given a "KERCHING!" figure of 16000 Rupees, she simply typed in her PIN and walked out of the shop with her lovely gifts.

Once the effects of the peanut cookies had worn off later in the day, she had a serious moment of, "Oh my good golly gosh, how much have I spent? How much is 16000 Rupees?!" Free WiFi at the Port revealed that it is $226. That's £172 on a few pungent vegetable substances used to flavour food and some oily rags. India 1: USA 0. KERCHING! KERCHING!

Next stop for Coach 14, a chance to "gaze at the ancient Chinese fishing nets that line the shores of Fort Kerching." As we are on 'Kerching At A Gallop,' 'gaze' was translated as 10 minutes to get to them from the coach and back, now the shopping was over. The tide was out, so the ancient Chinese fishing nets hung limply redundant over the shores of Fort Kerching. Fortunately, the Addams Family were still providing plenty of entertainment. The first sub plot involved Wednesday swapping places on Coach 14 with an unidentified member of the Addams Family, possibly Margaret Addams who was married to the Addams Family lawyer, Tully. You will appreciate that swapping places on an excursion is highly irregular, but we watched it unfold in front of us. As we walked back towards the coach, Wednesday was exiting stage left with Tully himself. We could not and still can't, understand who benefited from this exchange.

In that same moment we saw them disappearing, Morticia is quizzing Gomez on whether she has enough time to purchase a coconut and drink the contents. Not a man ever to say no, this was always going to happen. The next sighting of Morticia is her sucking out the contents of the coconut enthusiastically through a straw. Gomez enquires of her what it tastes like, perhaps in the vain hope he might be offered some. Whilst none is forthcoming, the quality line from Morticia is: "The one in Hawaii tasted better."

Next stop on Siad's Tour is a Catholic Church. The trouble with having well-travelled Cruisers in your Tour group is that they have been spoilt. Some of these Cruisers have seen the Seven Wonders of the World. A ramshackle Catholic Church in Kerching is a long way from the Great Pyramid of Giza. Some members of the Addams Family actually refused to go in. It was not clear whether this was because they didn't like religious sites, or they were bored, or whether they were afraid of being struck by lightning. Morticia did decide she could go in without getting struck down. She followed a now familiar pattern of wandering randomly around in a way that attracts a 'people watchers' eye. In this setting her wandering was so random that she actually physically bumped into Mrs F who was a little shocked. Moreover, it was not entirely clear whether her actions were accidental...

Having offered Mrs F psychological first aid, we followed Siad to an art gallery where we were to be served 'free refreshments.' On the way we had the joy of meeting Selwyn and his Carers who had already blitzed said refreshments and were outside waiting to depart on Coach 16. Selwyn got quite animated about the fact that his Tour Guide had done a runner on the back of a moped, leaving them stranded. Not quite sure whether to believe him or not, we swapped notes about our respective tours and the price of fish. Price of fish?! It's an old English phrase, "What's that got to do with the price of fish?" It's used when responding to a statement not in line with the general conversation, something which happened regularly when Selwyn was holding court. Suffice to say, that by the time we had established the price of fish when caught with an ancient Chinese fishing net in Fort Kerching, Tour Guide 16 had arrived back with her party. Selwyn was visibly relieved. A little too much so, actually. I wondered whether he had deployed his usual opening question to establish if she was single. Anyway, she explained that she had been to a local chemist to get some tablets for a member of Coach 16, which all sounded very laudable. Selwyn managed to put his tongue back in and followed her, rather too closely, back to the coach.

By the time we got past the shocking 'art' to the refreshment area, the Cruisers of Coach 14 were ready to leave. The locals kindly tried to ply us with various delicacies, but I resisted with the line, "No, that's really kind of you, but we can't afford to, they're making us fat on the ship." The eyes of the staff behind the counter rolled towards the members of Coach 14 sitting at the tables behind me. My eyes glanced over my shoulder to find 86 eyes boring into my soul with piles of empty cake cases sat in front of them on their tables. As the tumbleweed engulfed me, I raced back into the Gallery to try and find something interesting within the shocking art, whilst the rest of Coach 14 was embussing.

This was the final run now back to the cruise terminal in Kerching and the immigration rigmarole which we were becoming familiar with. As I got back onto the coach, trying desperately to avoid eye contact with those still with cake crumbs around their mouths, I heard a plaintive cry from Morticia: "Mummy can't find her Landing Card!" Grandmama Addams, who, to be fair to her, in our view had caused relatively little drama on this trip was to have the last hurrah. Within moments, the front end of the coach was being turned upside down in search of Grandmama's Landing Card. If they had thought about it, the Indian Government were unlikely to want to keep Grandmama Addams in The Marigold Hotel for the rest of her life. It was highly likely that a new Landing Card could have been drafted up within minutes. Seconds, if it was smoothed through with a few 'additional' Rupees.

The Addams Family take on life in some ways was quite refreshing. Every member of the Family bought into the drama and was fully committed to the search for Grandmama Addams Landing Card. Lurch even tried to introduce some order to the search process, but that was never going to happen. Siad was by now on the verge of a nervous breakdown. His 'Kerching At A Gallop' had been brought to a halt yet again. All his Tour Guide colleagues were texting him for a drink and he was still a long way from getting his old nags back to the stable. Siad tried in vain to get the Addams Family to sit down so the coach could drive off, but they were having none of it. Then he focussed on Margaret Addams who was standing at the front of the coach on her mobile talking to Tully about setting up legal arrangements for a new Landing Card. You could see Siad thinking, 'I am sure this woman was not on my tour when we started...'

If we were in England, it wouldn't have been long before other passengers' rumblings would have influenced the situation and we would have been on the move. However, the frenzied nature of the Addams Family activity seemed to mesmerise us remaining Cruisers and we all remained silent, as if this was perfectly normal.

Where do people store Landing Cards? Well, in this instance, no other member of the Addams Family was going to be able to find it. Apart from perhaps Grandad, who is dead, so that wasn't going to happen. Five minutes after announcing it was missing, Grandmama Addams announced she had found her own Landing Card. In the Chinese whispers which followed as the coach got underway, the informed view was that Grandmama Addams had stored her Landing Card intimately. This storage location is available to about 50% of the population and is one I am familiar with on account, as you have heard me whinging about, of living in a female dominated household. Usually, it is things like tissues that are stored there. I have, in a professional capacity you understand, been aware of ladies of the night storing fifty pounds notes there. But Landing Cards? That is a first. Grandmama Addams was sporting, what is known in the Lingerie Business as, a 'Sheepdog Bra' – round them up and gather them all in. Whilst space was tight, clearly there was enough room for a Landing Card next to Grandmama's bosom.

So, were we going to survive the journey back without any further Addams Family interference? I was hoping not, but had to wait until the final announcements from Siad as we pulled back into Kerching Cruise Terminal / Just tie your ship to a palm tree, Sir. Over the Tannoy, Siad said, (Been waiting for the whole Jackanory to type that) "… and one last very important announcement. The Head of Excursions from the Ship will be waiting at the port to speak to the occupants of Stateroom 666. Please can they make themselves known to her." Siad was looking, with a barely disguised grin on his face, at Gomez and then at Margaret Addams and back again. The whole of Coach 14 knew they had been found out.

Let me step briefly into the potentially litigious area of gender stereotypes. For years I have had to accept the allegation that, as a white Caucasian male, I have a hearing / listening / deafness problem. When I say 'accept,' in the course of a week I will be found guilty by Mrs F at least three times of allegedly not paying attention to an important detail of conversation. This has increased exponentially with age. It appears from my research with fellow downtrodden white Caucasian males, that this is a gender specific issue, a hearing / listening / deafness battle which no male, in a long term relationship, has ever won.

The battle I have won on behalf of the male gender relates to another sense, seeing / observing / blindness. For the Funn's, this began when we met on the back seat of a coach heading to… Morocco on holiday. Really?! Does this bloke just make it all up?

A coach trip to Morocco allows anyone remotely interested in wildlife the opportunity to see some amazing creatures. The only problem with wildlife is, that in order to survive, it moves. Over the course of the 52 hours it took us to get there, I identified that the future Mrs F had a severe seeing / observing / blindness problem. A white tailed sea eagle virtually flew in through the coach sun roof and she didn't see it.

Fast forward 28 years to our departure from Kerching along the river estuary towards the open sea. For the last week I had been banging on about NOT seeing any significant marine wildlife - like whales and dolphins. I had invested hours in scanning the horizon for said sighting. Nothing.

As we reached the last buoy before the ocean, whilst standing on our balcony (Did you realise we had one?), I delivered the following line for Mrs F's benefit:
"The Dolphin Display is a little late tonight Darling."
Not a murmur of appreciation. Betty would have been convulsing on the floor.

Not thirty seconds later the Dolphin Display was in full flow right in front of us. You could actually hear the local fisherman on the front of his boat shouting with excitement as at least three of them frolicked their way through the waves towards him.

At this point, even after 28 years of experience, I had made an assumption. The Dolphins were so obvious I had assumed Mrs F had seen them and said, "They are just so amazing aren't they. It was as if they heard what I said."
Mrs F: "What?"
I realised I had a problem and overcompensated:
"DOLPHINS! Look just behind the Fishing Boat - there, leaping out of the water, there... there, THERE..."
The combined power of nature and Foureyes Opticians could not help me. After repeated directions, pointing, Dolphins doing somersaults... Mrs F never saw them.
Mrs F never saw them.
Mrs F never saw them.

Why is this so painful to type? Why is it so frustrating that the person you love most in the world can't see what you can see? Why? Why? Why?

Probably for the same reason that I didn't hear that I was supposed to put the chicken in the oven.

It is probably the same frustration that God has, having put up so many signposts pointing towards Himself in creation.

DAY 10 – COLOMBO, SRI LANKA

My earthly Father kindly enquired, "How long after you left India did you feel like you could fart with confidence?" Well, nice of you to inquire Dad. Our colonic equilibrium remained stable on account of the fact that the only food we ate from India, as opposed to on the ship, was a cheeky little chocolate tart in Moonbucks, Mumbai. We took no risks. However, as Michael Schumacher once said, "No risk, no fun." It is therefore not something I am proud of. I accept that if you really want to experience a country and its culture, you need to eat there. But, by not eating anything Indian Dad, I continued to confidently do my bit to fill the ship with methane.

Arrival in Sri Lanka at midday cleared the way for a leisurely breakfast in the restaurant. Another chance to engage with Waiters and Waitresses from around the world. One of our favourite waiters was Sammy from... the Philippines? Really Sammy, is that a pseudonym? Apparently not. There is a generation of Philippians whose parents decided to give them western sounding first names. Sammy has been working for Cerebral Cruises for 21 years on a yearly rolling contract. Essentially he works 10 months solidly on the Ship... with no days off... perhaps a day or two when he doesn't have to work at breakfast or lunch... and then two months off, when Sammy returns to the Philippines, his wife and two children, 16 and 9 years in age. A very different lifestyle. On the Ship he shares a Cabin for 2 with a guy from India. Any issues Sammy? "Oh, he snores like a Harley Davidson." "Ah really, which model?"

After the obligatory laps of the ship, the sighting of land draws us to the foredeck to watch the approach into Colombo. As we make our way there we pass Selwyn in his now familiar sun-lounger and I shout, "Land ahoy!" Without taking breath Selwyn responds, "I thought we must be near, I saw a dove flying over." In the conversation which followed, it became clear that Selwyn's Carers had been calling into question Selwyn's Cruise CV. Consequently they had made some enquiries last night and got a print out of his Cruise history. Even at nearly eighty, you could see Selwyn's tail disappearing between his legs as his Carers began to wind the story up: "Yerr, so we managed to get the print out off him – how many Cruises do you think he has been on?"

Well, by the way Selwyn had been talking you would think he was in the Cruisers Half Century Club. He had certainly bored us regularly with his trip(s?) to Antarctica. Antarctica is the continent Cruisers talk in revered tones about – the Seventh Continent. It is a ginormous TICK on your Cruise CV, but it brings its own dilemma. As Cruisers have bored me, I will bore you. Or, as a Reader with free will, you might want to miss the next three paragraphs.

As a Cruiser, a member of the Flat Earth Society or even as an independent free thinker, if you have set foot on the six other Continents, a pervading obligation hangs over you to visit the seventh one before you become incontinent. The pressure to do so increases exponentially with age and the correlation with not being entirely sure how many heartbeats you have left. Once you make the decision you are going, an ethical question follows: Is going to see it enough, or do I need to set foot on Antarctica, to say with integrity, I have been there? The answer to this question is linked to the massive iceberg of cost. Much of your dependents inheritance melts away into the Southern Ocean if you choose to set foot on Antarctica.

Another consideration is that a visit there is linked with the ominous line, 'Most people that look into traveling to Antarctica are at the end of their adventures...'

...but that didn't stop 'about' 51,707 visitors to the Antarctic during the 2017/18 season, according to The International Association of Antarctica Tour Operators (IAATO). However, 9131 of them retained some of their dependents inheritance by not setting foot on Antarctica. I bet they are still bigging it up around the world saying they have visited all seven continents. Make sure you burst their bubble if you get the opportunity.

You will have realised that as Selwyn is at the end of his adventure and probably has less than 473 million heartbeats left. Having invested his children's inheritance heavily, he has taken no chances and got the Seven Continents ticked off on his Cruise CV. However, that does not answer the question about how many Cruises he has actually been on. As far as Cerebral Cruises were concerned, he had been on eight and a half. Well, whilst that was eight more than us, he certainly hadn't broken into the Cruisers Half Century Club. We listened to some flannel about other Cruise providers, but his Carers were having none of it. Asking Selwyn whether he wanted us to call his ex-wife to get a figure from his 'beloved' soon made him change the subject.

Having watched Captain Stavros dock us safely in Colombo Harbour, we began to prepare for our next excursion, 'Captivating Colombo.' The first burning question was whether the Addams Family would be joining us. Well they were certainly in the Cerebral Theatre. We picked up our stickers for Coach 19 and as I wandered down the Theatre aisle I passed Gomez briefing Uncle Fester.
Gomez: "Uncle this is your sticker, we are Number 16."
Uncle Fester pulled up his shirt and twisted it over to look at the sticker and said, "Well I'm Number 91."
Gomez was in for a long day... and unfortunately, we wouldn't be on board to support him.

Headmaster Seb was actually witnessed getting a hard time from a Cruiser unsatisfied with their itinerary. Having tried hard to placate them, he went for the good old, someone else will know approach:

"The tour operator will know."

Cruiser: "So should you."

No amount of Mexican charm was going to get him back from that one. He sent Coach 19 on its way and everyone filed off the Ship like clockwork.

The abiding memory of leaving the Port in Coach 19 was looking to our left and seeing Chair Buster Sid and his wife Nancy waddling along the top deck of an open top bus. However, this was no ordinary Tour Bus, this was Sri Lanka's one and only PARTY BUS. It was well and truly blinged up, massive speakers everywhere, lurid colours and music so loud the bus was rocking. Sid manoeuvred his quadruplets into place in the front seat of the top deck ready to PARTY! On their own, as there was no one else on the top deck.

I don't know what the state retirement age in Sri Lanka is, but our Tour Guide Sunil was well past it. If you were searching for positives, Sunil bought experience to the party: he was there when it was a British Crown colony between 1815 and 1948. It was then called Ceylon and how close to 1815 Sunil was born, was the subject of much discussion on Coach 19. As you have already heard, it is Mrs F who is a professional at diagnosing illness at 50 metres. I needed no assistance in identifying that Sunil had been inhaling the smoke from various different leaves from circa 1929 onwards: as a consequence he had the most irritating cough. When that cough was magnified down a 1940's microphone in the confines of a coach, it was as if you were actually inside his voice box.

This led to a very disrupted commentary interspersed with some moments of comedy when he would be talking in Sinhalese to the driver and an assistant, thinking he wasn't talking into the microphone. I am quite sure it would have been a far more interesting commentary if those Sinhalese asides could have been interpreted: "What are we going to tell these Cruise

Muppets today boys? Do you think they will believe that the Red Mosque took 76 years to build? I'll try it..."

What Sunil made abundantly clear was that there were some VERY old buildings in Colombo, cough, splutter, yawn...

As we got into the city itself, the flow of commentary began to improve, see if you can follow this:

"...this is China Street actually, we had a lot of Chinese here [Sinhalese language exchange] Now we on the [cough] main street. Well known Sari Centre. All closed because of the new year... They have all the rights and everything... and everything from India and so err... OK now the name Ceylon changed in 1972. Oh that's a very old building. This is the tallest building what we have. That is also a very old building – YMCA – very old building built in 1910 during the days of British. Yer er Buddhist temple everywhere you go see Buddhist statue everywhere [cough] [laugh][Sinhalese language exchange] So this Colombo 2 area. We have temple [pause] left side. Ohh, this is Lotus Tower. Actually we haven't finished it yet. Now you see Salvation Army HQ, built during days of British..."

Sunil had by now completely lost his audience, apart from me as I was fascinated that someone was apparently paying Sunil for these ramblings. I have subsequently tried listening to myself and realised that most of what I speak is also complete gibberish. Full credit to Sunil though, for getting paid for it. And for getting excited about seeing Mango trees:

"...these are all India willow trees, now Colombo is famous for mango tree, once again you can see the temple [cough] on your right side now. Now we are getting close to Colombo 7 area known as Cinnamon Garden. British clear the area - there is a mango tree over there, there is a mango tree on your left side and another one on your right and another one on left... and there are a few more [cough] Mango trees over there. The Portuguese arrived and saw the mango trees and called the city Colombo as it had many 'Kola Amba', which means green mangoes. Another mango tree over there. Wherever you go in Colombo there are Mango trees - look over there…"

A genuinely interesting Sunil Fact was that Sri Lanka elected the first lady Prime Minister in the world in 1960. Sirimavo Bandaranaike served as prime minister three times and was the leader of the Sri Lanka Freedom Party. It is always good, as a supposedly enlightened westerner, to be reminded that we are not always first when it comes to championing human rights: Maggie didn't make Prime Minister until 1979. The first thing she did was take away my free school milk which used to come every morning at 11am, in a little glass bottle, with a silver metal foil top covered in Blue Tit sh1t. 'Milk Snatcher Thatcher' we called her. Amazing what bitterness seeps out on a tour of Sri Lanka.

Our tour with Sunil ended with a cough, no sorry, with an ominous factoid. If I understood him correctly, a substantial part of the Port City of Colombo has been 'leased' to China. Not that I didn't trust Sunil, but a brief sortie on the Internet reveals the scale of Sri Lanka's debt crisis. Apparently it is so bad, the Government doesn't even know how much it owes. A figure of $8 billion is banded around as being owed to China alone.

If Chair Buster Sid comes back here for another party with his quadruplets in a few years' time, I suspect it will be a very different place.

DAY 11 – AT SEA

Funny how information can change your day.

I awoke glad to (a) have therefore been asleep, and, (b) be alive. We might as well have been trying to sleep on a Water Bed such were the rocky conditions overnight in the middle of the Indian Comocean. Having awoken, I arose for the routine morning curtain opening ceremony accompanied by the National Anthem. The white horses were dancing in tune to 'God save the Queen' to which I added a new line, 'and this ship.' It was grim. The wind was buffeting the Ship relentlessly. As the white horses rose, the wind whipped the water off the top of their silky white manes... and the resulting oily dandruff lashed MY balcony.

No time to lament this apocalyptic scene from a Cruise Holiday Nightmare. Having carelessly lost yet another hour, we were under pressure to make it for the cut off time of 9am for a non-Zoo breakfast.

Spirits were just beginning to lift, when Mrs F decides to deliver THE information, gleaned from her morning dose of TV. No, this was not about Mother Theresa's epic fail in the Brexit Vote. Neither was it about her triumphant victory by 19 votes which means we are all entirely confident in her Government, which took place the night before.

As I exit the bathroom she says:
"You will be pleased to hear the nearest land is Banda Aceh."
"Why does that sound familiar?"
"It was the epicentre of the earthquake that triggered the Indonesian tsunami"
Mrs F was of course referring to the Boxing Day tsunamis of 2004

which killed an estimated 227,898 people in 14 countries.

Well THANK YOU my dear. That has consigned me to a Day At Sea anxiously watching the horizon for tsunamis...

Do rough seas reduce the immense intakes of food on a Cruise?

Not in the slightest.

The galley is actually in crisis management mode. The inventory of foodstuffs which have run out is increasing by the minute. This first came to our attention when Mrs F's nightly order of 'Extra Vegetables,' changed. The vegetable colours evolved from green, orange and white... to traffic lights – green, orange and red: the cauliflower had run out. Crisis. Mrs F dealt with the disappointment very maturely. She rejected the replacement tomato.

Next to fall were lemons.

One of the pampering rituals that greets Cruisers from their gruelling trips ashore, is a reception committee of staff housed next to the gangway in a line of gazebos. Cruisers are plied with flannels laced with ice to cool fevered brows. A line of chilled water options awaits, a choice of three: orange, plain or lemon infused.

It happened in Goa.

The lemon became grapefruit. Subtle as it was, it was noted. Our friendly Assistant Waiter Sivo cracked under heavy questioning. And when could we expect normal service to resume? Not until Singapore, Sir. Shocking. I stopped short of seeking some form of recompense for this major inconvenience ...and settled for another glass of grapefruit infused water.

It became even more serious when Mrs F tried to order bananas for breakfast. All gone. The breakfast menu shrunk again, from 1367 items to 1366.

So what would happen at Breakfast this morning? Well in the post Zoo era, it had become traditional to dine at a table for two. As you may have picked up, this was all a little farcical as more often than not there was a six inch / 15 centimetre gap between tables: it might as well have been a table for four. This led to some highly amusing transactions: are we going to engage with the adjoining couple, or not?

This mornings American couple fell into the 'or not' bracket. It was for their benefit and ours. I didn't want to hear about their Cruises' at 9am and they wouldn't have been blessed by me telling them about their need for Jesus.

The great thing about sitting six inches from someone and not talking to them is the free insight you get into their relationship.

To build a picture in your mind, this couple were well on their way to Deadweight. Both on account of their weight and their age. It rapidly became apparent that as far as Salvador was concerned, Cressida was in charge. Sal's breakfast was actually a briefing:
"Right, so, when we arrive in Singapore, you are going to go through customs. You are then going to go through arrivals. You are then going to pick up the rental car..."

...and so it continued, and bearing in mind Singapore was three days away, it was difficult to know when it was going to stop. Fortunately for Sal, the Waiter arrived.

Sal was empowered to select his own breakfast.
"I would like 10 to 12 prunes."
Waiter: "Not 9 to 11?"
Sal: (Complete sense of humour failure) "No, 10 to 12."
Waiter: (Winks at Mrs F) "Would you like anything else?"
Sal: "Two slices of wholemeal bread and <u>half</u> an eggs Benedict.'
Waiter: "Certainly Sir."

The briefing from Cressida continues, but is interrupted by the arrival of Round 1.

Waiter: "Sir, the 10 prunes you ordered. I have counted them."

Sal completely blanked him. Waiter winks at Mrs F.

Briefing moves onto how Sal should be eating.

"Use the big spoon. ...the small spoon is for stirring your coffee. ...that's it, finish your toast..." ...and so it continued. I have never witnessed anything like it. It was like 'How to eat' coaching on our floating rest home.

After we had had a few more exchanges with the Winky Waiter about balancing the benefits of eating melon v Canadian bacon, Sal was finally being allowed to speak.

It became apparent that both Sal and Cressida had been married before and for some reason this morning they had decided to fill in a few gaps in their respective histories. The Topic matter? Cruising of course.

Sal: "I can't remember that."

Cress: "Well I certainly did a Cruise from the Caribbean half way through the Panama Canal."

Sal: "Well I did a Cruise all the way through the Panama Canal."

Cress: "Well that must have been before we met."

Sal: "You think we weren't together then?"

Cress: "Well I only went half way through."

...and so it went on...

As you would expect, when we met Selwyn on our rounds of the Mortuary Deck, he had a view on this. Firstly he was impressed by the fact Sal had eaten ten prunes. "Cor, they would have a catastrophic effect on me..." Secondly, he does love a good Cruising story old Selwyn and mention of the Panama Canal pushed one of his buttons.

It led him to tell us about his previous evening, when he claimed to have entertained two young women. We clarified that 'young' for Selwyn was under 70. Apparently he had tried to woo them by sharing tales of the Panama Canal and his experience on 8 ½ Cruises. Sadly, he was blown out of the water by one of them who had done 56... Selwyn remains single.

The travesty of the day was that it had taken 10 days of wobbling about on this large cork, to discover that they serve a sumptuous Afternoon Tea at 4pm. If ever that dubious phrase 'Nice spread' was appropriate, it was to summarise what treats lay in front of us. After all these days of all-inclusive living, Mrs Funn was now a little out of control, if I'm honest, when faced with this kind of opportunity. She adopted the recognised 'Harvester Salad Bowl Methodology' – build it as high as you can. However, she completely forgot that in the Food Zoo scenario it's free: you can go up as many times as you like.

Her plate resembled a multiple car pile up. There were scones, cakes, eclairs, cream, jam, butter, cookies... don't worry, I sent a picture to her Slimming Universe Consultant.

As we headed outside with Mrs F's plate balanced on a sack barrow, I spotted B6 on her own enjoying a quiet beer overlooking the aft / rear / ass end of the Ship. Believing that Funn always overrules reflection, we wrecked her afternoon by joining her.

As we did so, Mrs F was clearly suddenly overwhelmed with guilt and began insisting that B6 sampled a scone. You may recall that B6 is a Psychiatrist and would therefore have clearly recognised that Mrs F was 'projecting' her guilt onto her. Despite protestations to the contrary, B6 found herself with a fully loaded scone in her hand on the basis it was a British tradition, and she NEEDED to try it. After the usual, "So will you be cruising again?" routine, yawn, it became apparent that B6 was planning to go to 'Improv.' Never heard of it? Neither had we. Improv is apparently all the rage in North America and is short for Improvisational Comedy.

We had a standing joke with B6 about choices. Whether an entertainer was 'worth' going to see, versus, whether you 'wanted' to go. She had developed a five minute rule; any form of entertainment would be given five minutes for her to assess whether it was 'worth' staying for. Even it was 'worth' it, she then made a choice about whether she 'wanted' to stay. As we had seen her walk out on a singer after five minutes the previous night, we were on the front foot. Much hilarity was derived from watching her trying to justify this, in our view, brutal assessment. We were coming from a position of not having missed the evening entertainment for 9 nights in a row and going for a full house... which raises a really disturbing question: 'Have I been turned: am I starting to enjoy Cruising?'

Well 'Improv' was to suggest otherwise. We dutifully trudged down to a venue in the Ship we had not graced with our presence before. The lighting was dim and the initial working hypothesis was the audience were to... and that of course includes me. At the front already working hard to raise a few titters, were an American couple. Whether that is a good start or not is a matter of an individual opinion. I am 'Diversity Trained' and from a public service background, so come at these sorts of issues very open mindedly...

The subject matter is puns. An example is given. 'One hundred and eighty five penguins walk into a bar. The barman says...' The example was so bad, I can't even remember it.

The play is then made of selecting a variety of 'things' that the audience then suggest to replace penguins. First up is 'monkeys.' 'One hundred and eighty five monkeys walk into a bar. The barman says...'
You will rapidly appreciate this kind of humour is only as good as the facilitators and the audience...
Well I was poor, and the facilitators were appalling.

Next up, three chairs at the front for three 'volunteers'. The best part of this act was that no-one volunteered. No-one. Our

American Facilitator, I am not gracious enough to call him a Comedian, thought someone stood up to volunteer and rushed over to greet him. The guy was trying to leave... and got the biggest round of applause for doing so.

Never has a trip to the Gym seemed so appealing.

Mr and Mrs no Funn were next to leave. Sorry B6, they weren't 'worth' any more of our 1440 minutes today.

We had begun to observe that we were always placed in a certain area of the Restaurant whatever time we arrived. We quizzed Josie from Kenya, the Maître d', about how she allocated our table. It transpires the Table Intelligence – where you have been seated on all your previous visits to the Restaurant is stored and she utilises it to seat you in the same area, so you get the same Waiting Staff. Having established this we decided we would like to go on a Table Vacation – a tour through the Restaurant to meet different staff: we drew the line at different Cruisers – the wounds from Table Roulette were still too raw.

This meant we moved on Night 1 from Port to Starboard with a table for two next to the window. What on earth were we going to talk about? We had now been together for 28 years, married for 26 and spent the last six months together every day.

Well, I have learnt in that time, if you haven't got any problems to talk about yourself, talk about someone else's. The couple on a table for two, three metres away were having a right old barney. Unfortunately, the subject matter of the barney was not clear as I was busy having, in my view, a humorous exchange with our new Waiter. The barney ended with the immortal words from the woman, "I do NOT have to explain my reasoning to YOU." It all went silent. Not just on their table, but for a radius of three tables around them. Gradually conversations resumed, but they sat in silence for the rest of their meal.

We had a thoroughly enjoyable meal together with me explaining my reasoning for finding it so amusing that she felt she did not have to explain her reasoning to him. After a quick dessert, off we trotted off like a pair of sheep to the Cerebral Theatre for our Evening Entertainment. We were now firmly in the Cruising Groove: 'Resistance is futile' and all that.

Tonight we were promised a comedy show with no words. Interesting. Humour in mime. Essentially it was a couple of blokes' pratting around on stage with a few props which got a mixed reaction from Cruisers. Schoolboys like me loved it. However, the stand out 'performer' was a member of the audience. Shane was picked out from the middle of Row 6 of the audience. Row 6?! Shouldn't you be safe in Row 6? I think it was because he was the only bloke under 70. After his wonderful performance, others thought he was a plant.

Shane was coerced onto the stage without any words being used, after pretending to fire a peashooter at the two blokes. That in itself deserved a round of applause. He was then stood in the middle of the two blokes and given a piece of paper. The premise was that Shane was required to copy what the blokes were doing which he dutifully did. Firstly it was to become a baton and much slapstick followed as they whacked each over with said baton... the baton was then tweaked into a skirt with the obligatory dance and pirouette ... which became pom-poms. The only thing Shane couldn't match them like for like, was a cartwheel. We forgave him that and gave him a standing ovation.

DAY 12 – PHUKET, THAILAND

At our table for two in the post zoo diner, we were served by Servde from India. Now that we had tuned in to length of service, we established Servde had served for 17 years. We enquired about his family and he has three children, 15, 8 and 3. There was a slight silence from Mrs F after his reply which allowed him to deliver his clearly well-rehearsed line, "Every time I go home, I make another one."

As we sailed into Phuket a new challenge awaited us, transfer by Tender – which Selwyn informed me is nautical term for a smaller boat used for transporting Cruisers to and from shore. This meant dropping anchor in Patong Bay, which we steamed into like Captain Stavros owned it. Captain Stavros was particularly miffed by a Thai fishing boat which looked like it was on a collision course with us. Stavey gave it the BIG one on his Foghorn. This had two direct effects. Firstly the Thai fishing boat stopped dead in its tracks. Secondly, those brave enough to be on the Mortuary Deck in the inclement conditions, were raised from the dead.

After a leisurely lunch, the Funn's sauntered down to the Cerebral Theatre ready for Headmaster Seb's, 'Pucker Phuket.' This time he put us on an Addams Family free, Coach 14. Boonsri was our guide for the next 5 ½ hours for which she talked for 329 minutes. This would have been alright, but we were delayed a further hour. Fortunately her script ran out, so she only talked for a further 58 minutes. Boonsri wasn't tongue-Thaied, I'll give her that.

As I had become progressively more cynical about Tour Guides as the Cruise went on, the first fact Boonsri delivered that had me consulting Boogle, related to population. Boonsri reckoned that the population of Phuket Island was 200k and in the high season around Christmas it swelled to a million. Boogle reckons that the population of Phuket Island is 600k and in the high season around Christmas it swelled to over a million.

Boonsri's credibility was further knocked by the claim, "We created the Lord Buddha." That is a pretty bold claim Boonsri, what exactly do you mean by that? Well, by way of qualification Boonsri pointed towards the schoolchildren in Thailand: "They learn about Buddha for ten years... you have half an hour." Fair point, but I am still fairly sure the origins of the late great Lord Buddha are in ancient India... having said that, Chair Buster Sid's view probably ought to be sought on this. Further apparent blasphemy followed later when she suggested Lord Buddha was born under the cannon ball tree. If she had suggested he had eaten an almighty cannon ball, which his one pack suggests, I might have been able to believe her. It's no wonder people are struggling to know who to place their faith in these days.

I have distilled the next five hours of commentary into Boonsri's Top 3 interesting facts about Thailand:
1. Scooters are more dangerous than sharks.
2. The colourful sea urchins you can see on the beaches are like beautiful girls, very dangerous.
3. Boonsri is banned by the Thai Government from talking about politics on the tour.

I can assure you that by the end of the tour, as you are about to find out, politics was the only topic Boonsri didn't talk about.

We did actually have some stops on this excursion, five in total. Three related to Temples, one was a Museum (With free WiFi, so not all bad) and the fifth pressed that all important Cruisers Food Button – a Cashew Nut Factory. A famous one, apparently. How Cerebral Cruises distinguishes between an ordinary

Cashew Nut Factory and a famous one, I can offer no insight.

You won't be at all surprised to hear that Selwyn beat us to the Famous Cashew Nut Factory on Coach 16. Is Selwyn always on Coach 16? Good question. I asked him, but he thought he was on Coach 91.

The next question was, now that Selwyn's been, will there be any cashew nuts left? Well one of Selwyn's lines was, "Are you feeling hungry?" "Yes." "That's good, coz there's lots of different flavours of FREE cashew nuts in there." Selwyn was not wrong. And I did not leave hungry. But I did leave a few Thai Bahts lighter. You can't beat a bit of Bahter with Selwyn.

What did we actually learn at the Cashew Nut Factory? Firstly that cashew nuts grow on trees. The fruit is boxing-glove shaped drupe that grows at the end of the cashew apple and contains a single nut... this nut is extracted from the drupe by hand... all of which starts to explain why I was so many Bahts lighter at the end of my visit. What we didn't learn and why Boogle is a bad thing, is that the romantic view I had that cashew nuts were unique to Thailand and that is why the factory was so famous... was wrong: Boogle says cashew nuts are native to Brazil. So, the Famous Cashew Nut Factory was really just another shop to fleece foreigners, where the Tour Guide gets a bung for taking you there. Always good to have some more evidence to reinforce ones cynicism.

Honey coated cashew nuts, free, by the handful, still taste nice though.

On the excursion blurb, we were promised a visit to see The BIG Buddha. Having had Chair Buster Sid on the Cruise, I did wonder whether we needed to. However, Boonsri was all very enthusiastic about it, so we transferred from Coach 14 to Minibus 143. Minibus 143 was an object of desire, it had been lovingly blinged up. The passenger ceiling had 'Louis Vuitton' (Apparently a French fashion house) emblazoned all over it with an ever changing light display behind it. Time to compliment the Driver, but first the precautionary check: "Hi, do you speak English?" Without a milliseconds hesitation he said, "No." I laughed and carried on speaking English more loudly... but the Driver was having none of it. Silence all the way up the hill to The BIG Buddha.

You might recall my view that most of the world's concrete is in Abu Dhabi. Well, it appears that an A380 Airbus full of concrete on the way to Abu Dhabi crashed vertically into the ground on the top of a hill in Phuket. Before the concrete dried, they made some primitive attempts to shape it into a Buddha and still haven't finished the work on it yet, five years later. My Primary School Teacher, Mrs Ewans would have summed it up in red pen as, "Could do better."

After being Templed Out, we started to head back towards the boat. Owing to some roadworks we ended up running an hour late. Boonsri had lulled the majority of Coach 14 to sleep, until we got to a road which happened to have a renowned Cabaret on it called, 'Simon's.' Well, it hopefully won't surprise you that I have not heard of it, but I would be intrigued to know if you have. Boonsri assured us Simon's has been successful for more than two decades. Apparently, there should be no need to tell you what makes Simon's Cabaret so famous. It's not the exclusive, luxurious and intimate theatre with hi-tech sound. It's not the light equipment costumes or the unforgettably glamorous performers. It's not the stage design or the plethora of feathers. It's not even the performance.

Coach 14 was now awake again. Boonsri's tone had changed, she was getting excited. She realised she had got her audience back and she was hamming it up: "Ladies and Gentlemen, Simon's is all about the Ladyboys phenomenon!" Pause to allow audience to catch up. Boonsri realised that this theoretically devastating reveal had not quite had the impact on her audience she was expecting. She had not properly assessed Coach 14's demographic. Consequently she introduces the word 'transvestite' into the Coach: that got EVERYONES attention. Especially when you float the idea that Simon's Cabaret can certainly afford the prettiest ones.

Now for the majority on the coach, that would have been quite enough about Simon's. Thank you very much Boonsri, and Good Night.

Boonsri had other ideas. For some inexplicable reason she decided it was her duty as a Thai Tour Guide to tell us in explicit detail about how you might consider becoming a Ladyboy. Well, for a start this career option was only open to about fifty percent of the coach. As a white, Anglo Saxon, six foot plus, middle aged male I am willing to disclose that becoming a Ladyboy was not presented to me as a career option by my Careers Advisor, Mr Morris, in the sixth form. It maybe in 2019, but I am not entirely sure whether Prince Henry's High School has risen to that level of inclusivity yet.

One other topic I have spared you from to date is Medical Tourism. This is a phrase I had not tuned into until becoming a Cruiser. In various places it is becoming BIG business and in Thailand everything is on the (operating) table: cosmetic surgery, weight loss surgery, dentistry, fertility treatment… Apparently, although it now shares the spotlight with India, Singapore, and Malaysia, Thailand is the 'rightful wellspring of contemporary medical tourism.'

Boonsri was about to outline Thailand's medical options in forensic detail. The only semi reasonable quote I can attribute to her without you all shutting this book, is: "You see Ladyboys, it's not only about the boob job right?"

Her commentary went South from there on. Literally South. Operations are available I didn't even know could be considered. Boonsri covered them all leaving the occupants of Coach 14 wincing, blushing and blocking their ears. How the parents of Francesca aged 9 on Row 3, were going to explain this all to her later, I have no idea. Boonsri just kept going and bizarrely, no one felt able to stop her. Surely she has finished now? "…and if you want to, you can have it..." And the prices as well?! I am sure Boonsri was on commission, it was like she was reading it all off a Medical Tourist Brochure.

As if that wasn't enough, we then got a warts and all history of Transvestites in Thailand. Followed by how to compete in a Ladyboys Beauty Pageant. I had already had my fill of Buddhist enlightenment on this excursion, but this was taking it a bit far. Having said that, Boonsri had told us that Buddhists believe a person can become enlightened by following the Middle Way. Perhaps Sirirat Rd, Phuket, was the Middle Way? I don't know, but I was extremely glad to get off Coach 14 at the end of Sirirat Road. Wait a minute, does that mean I am in Nirvana? After my half an hours input on Buddhism, I was not qualified to answer that.

There was a Spirit of Dunkirk on the pontoon in Patong Bay. Coach 14 was not the only excursion stuck in the eternal traffic jam along Middle Way. As we walked from the coach and arrived at the entrance to the pontoon, a party of Cerebral Angels heralded our return as if we were lost explorers, last seen on the Great Wall of China. Hundreds of weary Cruisers lined up respectfully awaiting the arrival of the next Tender. More Cerebral Cherubs mopped our fevered brows with ice cold flannels. Sherman, the 96 year old Great British Grandfather of Francesca from Row 3, took 'flannelling' to a whole new level. He placed his flannel into both cupped palms in front of him, leant forward slightly and thrust the flannel into his face, rubbing vigorously, gnawing at his gnarled jowls. Not satisfied with the cleansing effect, he then worked upwards, covering his forehead and then enveloped his head with the flannel and continued to rub robustly. I was mesmerised. The net effect was that a 96 year old bog brush appeared from underneath the flannel and presented itself upright on the pontoon. Several white bristles detached themselves from Sherman's scalp and fluttered away into the warm evening breeze. The remaining bristles were aggressively styled with his right hand into a side parting that could loosely pass as a comb over. Sherman then marched up the gangplank, head held high, stiff upper lip, onto the Tender, just as he did 78 years ago in Dunkirk. What a Trooper.

DAY 13 – AT SEA

Having promoted Breakfast in the Restaurant to Selwyn's Carers, Samson and Delilah, they allowed him to dine with us, which meant the day was always going to start well. The conversation began with a debrief on the day before, with a conscious effort not to remind Selwyn about the Ladyboys. Initially it became a competition about which Coach, 14 or 16, had the most talkative guide. This raised the challenge of how do you talk up a talkative guide to make them seem more talkative than someone else's talkative guide who you have not heard talk. Not for the first time, Selwyn and I agreed to disagree about who's guide was the most verbose.

Next up was the Famous Cashew Nut Factory. You will recall that we met them there and Selwyn prophesied, correctly, that we would not leave feeling hungry. However, we established that the biggest winner in the Free Cashew Nut Fest was Samson. He ate everything, spent nothing and left thinking he had been eating pistachio nuts.

We were than treated to the story about how Samson and Delilah met on a blind date, having now been married for 52 years. They had been set up by 'friends' to meet, according to Samson, in The Wheatsheaf Pub. He started to talk effusively about the table they met at, the flower arrangement... until he was interrupted by Delilah: "No you have forgotten, we actually met beforehand in the Samson Hotel. We then went on to The Wheatsheaf." Samson was astounded. He had had over 52 years to get this story straight and he had fluffed his lines. After initial protestations, he conceded defeat. Having endured the rest of the tale, I commented, "Amazing to think Delilah that you met a bloke called Samson on a Blind Date in the Samson Hotel." They both went silent. "That has never occurred to me," said Samson. That's probably because Delilah's cut your hair off again Samson.

The final smile in the Restaurant as we were leaving, was seeing a family arriving who had clearly missed all the announcements that the clocks went forward one hour overnight. They were turned away to fight for their own survival in the Food Zoo.

We were now entering the twenty four hours after which I would never be Cruising again in my life. Mrs F has a contrary view. Do you think we will be Cruising together again? The twenty four hour marker means of course, that you are starting to do everything for the last time.

It was therefore the last 10am Tannoy Announcement. Fortunately I had managed to get Mrs F seated before Captain Stavros started talking. You could hear the emotion in his voice as he bid us, 'Good Morning Cruisers.' He must have done this a thousand times, the final Tannoy Announcement, but there must be at least one powerpoint about it at Captains' School. Captain Stavros had swallowed the slides because he made it sound genuinely painful that he was going to have to say goodbye tomorrow. Tears started rolling down Mrs F's cheeks.

He lurched back into the daily patter of weather conditions, 18 knots and then added a questionable fact: "We are currently in the Strait of Malacca (CORRECT), which is the shortest route between the Pacific and Indian oceans (CORRECT). It is 550 miles wide (CORRECT) and links the major Asian economies (CORRECT). The Strait of Malacca is the world's busiest shipping lane (INCORRECT)."

No, Captain Stavros, Boogle says the English Channel is the world's busiest shipping lane. So does the Guinness Book of Records. Currently, approximately 500 ships travel the channel daily and there will be even more going past us and not stopping after Brexit.

Do you remember the time Captain Stavros first used the words which follow? Well he used them again to sign off his final 10am Tannoy Message. Please remember to read them in the euphonious tones of a Greek God:

"Remember life is beautiful, enjoy every moment of it."

Don't be surprised if you wake up reading this wondering where the last half an hour went. Two hypotheses: One, you were so bored your eyes had no other option. Two, you to have become a subject of Captain Stavros's worldwide hypnotic powers.

This would be the last day we saw Sally, the Stair, Lift and Lobby Cleaner. Sally was from the Philippines and a sheet of A4 short of four feet. She had a chameleon like ability to blend into her surroundings which in a stairwell is quite something. If you weren't observant, you could pass her without noticing she was busy cleaning anything and everything. Mrs F made a particular fuss of Sally, but the reality was that here on the last day of our Cruise, we still did not know anything about her. She couldn't speak any English, we couldn't speak any Flippingo. Communication with Sally was all about laughter, hand gestures and head nodding. Sally probably thought we were several sandwiches short of a Cerebral Cruises picnic.

My last abiding memory of Sally was seeing her extending her almost four foot frame to its full extent with a most ingenious dusting contraption outstretched in her right hand. The purpose of this effort was to clean the top of a glass cabinet which was replicated on every one of the eleven levels in the three stairwell lobbies on the Ship, thirty three in all. This was clearly part of Sally's weekly routine and she was completing it all very methodically. She was a great Cleaner.

#loveyourcleaner

Where we are going next is what was actually in the glass cabinets. What do you put in thirty three glass cabinets on an allegedly Five Star Cruise Liner? Well in the absence of anything useful, 'art' of course.

What is 'art'?

'Art' is a matter of opinion and, as you might have noticed, I am not short of an opinion. I certainly have an opinion on what Cerebral Cruises decided to put in their glass cabinets.

A lady had apparently got some clay out of a bag on a wet Thursday in 1961 and put it on her kitchen table; she smeared and poked her fingers into it; went out shopping; returned, poured some honey over the dry clay and put it in the oven; went out shopping again; returned, removed the clay from the oven and displayed it on a square bit of cardboard. In your imagination you simply need to visualise a random pile of beige clay about ten inches (25 centimetres) high. A more contemporary visualisation would be the poo emoji. Here is the unbelievable bit. She then got someone from Cerebral Cruises to pay money for it. An undisclosed sum of money. Not just for one, but for eleven – enough to fill the Midships Stairwell glass, blooming, cabinets.

Having enjoyed four of these wonderful piles of ordure between Decks 7 and 10, I went in search of Scott and Bailey, to establish whether our final 11.30am game of Scrabble was on or not. Scott confirmed Her Majesty, HRH Bailey, would be available to receive guests this morning. I scuttled off to find Mrs F who had adopted a sunny alcove on Deck 12. On the way there, I clocked Shane from Row 6, languishing in a sunlounger.

Once Mrs F was mobile, we approached Shane on the way back and I woke him up with the line, "Sorry I don't want to disturb your sunbathing, but can I have your autograph."

Bearing in mind he had been asleep and we had never met me before, Shane was on it: "Ah, you are not the first person to ask me that!" An animated, we've known each other for life, conversation sprung up. Shane explained that he was with his mother on the Cruise and felt they should have been safe in Row 6 attending a comedy show with no words. We showered him with compliments about his performance. Shane was the kind of guy we wished we had met earlier on the Cruise and now we were under 'pressure' to make our Scrabble date. We advised him to get an agent and left him to catch some final rays before returning to London at -1°C.

HRH Bailey was in a particularly chatty mood and not shy in sharing a few opinions. She was particularly impressed by a 61 year old man who kept walking past on the jogging track we were next to, in the smoking area. There was nothing unusual about him, apart from the fact he was wearing nothing apart from a small piece of black Lycra to maintain his modesty. It was an interesting symbiosis. HRH Bailey benefitted visually from his regular walk pasts; he benefitted nasally from her cigarette smoke each time he passed.

Unfortunately, Scott had informed HRH Bailey that I had been in the police. Periodically she would make irritating references to this like, "People always think I am in the CID." How do you respond to that?
1. "How interesting, I can see why."
2. "More chance of you being investigated by the CID luv."
3. Silence.

I couldn't decide whether to use 1. and lie; use 2. and not play Scrabble, so I went with 3.

Even Jesus used silence. He gave the first ever recorded 'No comment' interview to Pontius Pilate, governor of Judea who presided over his trial. The difference here was Jesus was crucified and I carried on playing Scrabble.

Of all the marvellous asides we had whilst playing Scrabble in the Smoking Area, meeting all HRH Bailey's CID colleagues, one of my favourite images was Sully the crapulent Canadian. Sully the sozzled, sidled up to our Scrabble table. You didn't have to be a CID Detective to observe things were not well in Sully's world. It was half past midday and these are your other

Scooby's: Unkempt hair; Dark glasses; Stubble; Crumpled Guinness T shirt; Mug of coffee in right hand; Glass of water in his left. Sully had been getting value for money out of his drinks package.

HRH Bailey greeted him in a piercingly shrill voice, "Good night then Sully?" Sully visibly winced and after a delay said, "...ohh yes, just got up. Great night... had my best night's sleep on the ship." Sully shuffled off and HRH Bailey raised her eyebrows and muttered, "One night to go."

The best thing that happened Scrabble wise was that the much maligned Scott won the last game. A great finale with a couple who had been a ray of sunshine on the Erudite.

After a couple of bulgur wheat salads (?) from the Food Zoo, it was time to squeeze our last bit of value out of our balcony. Did I mention we had one?

On the way back to our Stateroom we bumped into Selwyn who couldn't wait to meet up with us at 4pm for Afternoon Tea. He was getting quite carried away with himself. At one point he said, "I've got a question for you." I jumped in, "Selwyn, keep it for later, otherwise we will run out of things to talk about." We agreed he would remember the question and we went our separate ways.

The next person we bumped into was another woman, on a growing list, who had rejected Selwyn's advances. B6 was sitting alone and reflecting on a strange chain of events she had just had in the Restaurant over lunch:

"So I was on a table with five of us for lunch, two Brits and a Canadian couple. The Canadian's had had a few jibes about the usual things, Trump, the wall and I had let them go over my head. They then started talking about American health care and the guy says, "Isn't it a shame that you have a health care system that doesn't care for its citizens." Well I decided that I would give a contrary view in defence of our system. The Canadian couple became really argumentative and after a few minutes I found myself saying, "Well I'm on a cruise, I didn't come here for an argument, I'm leaving." He says, "Well good – beat it!" I lost it and said, "Well screw you!" and he says, "Screw you to!" and as I walk away he shouts, "Yeah beat it!" I am still fuming trying to get my head round it."

We talked it through and I asked the inevitable question about whether her role as a Psychiatrist helped her cope with this kind of incident. B6 very honestly explained that when she was on holiday she left all her training at home. Psychiatrists appear to be human.

However much you pay for something, it is inevitable that things go wrong. Today the toilet decided to malfunction. This sent me in search of a privy in a public area I was rarely seen in, mid-afternoon. Consequently, I stumbled into my first Art Auction.

Why would you hold an art auction on a Ship in the middle of The Strait of Malacca with a maximum of 2146 buyers and peasants like me on board? What do I know? This is not the first one and it is clearly a regular event on Cerebral Cruises.

The Auctioneer had begun his spiel to 17 assembled Cruisers using the obligatory PowerPoint presentation. He was starting to expound the opportunity Cruisers had to pick up a unique piece of art and already a number of Cruisers had begun to drift off. Why had they bothered attending? Was this just an alternative venue to sleep off the effects of the Food Zoo? Maybe. It all then became clear. "…and I hope you are thirsty because we have some free champagne for you." Upon hearing this uplifting news, the man in front of me switched off his hearing aid and shut his eyes. Respect. This was clearly a seasoned campaigner in a(u)ction. There was no doubt he had played this art auction game before. At least 45 minutes afternoon nap. Wake up. Switch your hearing aid back on. Await the last item in the auction. Claim free champagne. Quaff accordingly. Depart.

Having realised the poo emoji's were tragically not in the auction, I too departed.

The highlight of the day was always going to be Afternoon Tea with Selwyn at 4pm. You will recall that our previous Afternoon Tea involved Selwyn's ex… table neighbour, B6. We had spoken in such glowing terms about our Afternoon Tea experience that Selwyn and his Carers agreed to join us to sample the fare.

It didn't disappoint. An endless honeycomb of scones, lashings of cream, plump succulent strawberries suspended in jamminess, Belgium chocolate enveloped eclairs… Mrs F's Slimming Universe Consultant would have loved it. The truth is most Consultants are 'Ex' Food Addicts, who like Christians, preach the Doctrine of 'Sins.' In Christianity, 'sin' means 'to miss the mark.' The mark, in this case, is the standard of perfection established by God and evidenced by Jesus. In a Slimming Universe context, a 'sin' is a minor transgression into the realm of the calorific. I must remember to ask Mrs F whether a Slimming Universe Consultant has the power to forgive 'sins.'

Selwyn fell into the same trap as Mrs F did and loaded his plate until it looked like a model of the Burj Khalifa. He was remarkably quiet as he munched his way through the 163 floors. Both he and I knew we were building up to THE question. Selwyn's Carers and Mrs F were waiting expectantly. Why is it when someone precedes their question with, "I've got a question for you," you instinctively think it is going to be a soul searching, insightful, thought provoking, separating bone from marrow type of question. Selwyn's Pantomime experience had taught him to ham things up and he had now been waiting three hours to deliver this verbal hand grenade.

When he reached the third floor, he couldn't wait any longer. He pulled the pin out and said, "OK. I've got a question for you. What school did you go to?"

As anti-climaxes go in my life, this was straight into my Top 10.

Knowing that he really wanted to hear that I went to a posh private school, I gave him this response: "Brook County Primary School, Selwyn. 34 pupils ranging from 5 to 11. Headmaster Mr T.E. Wood. Sheltered upbringing me."

Selwyn actually looked crestfallen. His Carers got on board and threw a few punches. Even the lovely Mrs F questioned the quality of his question.

After some brave talk of a final game of Table Roulette, we enjoyed our last dinner on the Erudite on a table for two. Why is that a bad thing? There is nothing to write about.

DAY 14 – SINGAPORE
7AM DEBARK

Having been to Singapore ten years ago, I was excited about returning. So excited I awoke at 5.45am and had a final seat on our balcony in the darkness as we entered Singapore Harbour. The Erudite already had a tug boat attached to her ass to keep her on course. I gave the tug boat Captain the full benefit of my white napkin and brown socks.

Two things make the entrance to Singapore notable. The Singapore Flyer is a giant Ferris wheel 165 metres high lit 24/7. To its left as we approached is the Five Star Marina Bay Sands Hotel. This has three, 55 storey towers linked on top by the SkyPark, a three-acre park on top of the building with a 146 metre infinity pool, 191 metres above the ground. Goodness, you will be thinking, some facts after all this blaaa. Too little, too late to become a Travel Writer now.

The best finale Cerebral Cruises could offer? Breakfast with Selwyn.

Cruisers exit from the Ship was very carefully orchestrated and our allotted disembarkation time was 9.40am. We had agreed to meet at 8am in the Restaurant and his Carers delivered him accordingly. As we arrived at the table, all was not well. Selwyn was in some discomfort. Samson and Delilah explained, with some glee in their voices, that they had been given a bottle of champagne last night as part of their package. As they hadn't finished it, they had given it to Selwyn. Selwyn decided it would be a good idea to decant the champagne into his water bottle for transportation purposes. What he didn't realise is that the bottle was leaking… so as he arrived at breakfast he discovered it had soaked everything in his rucksack… and leaked out down the back of his trousers giving the impression he had had a bladder malfunction. For a man only too willing to tell you he had several Urology Consultants, this was a proper waterworks crisis. Needless to say, the four others of us on the table were very sympathetically in danger of having similar mishaps owing to excessive laughter. After a considerable amount of faffing around with numerous serviettes, Selwyn decided to go find a drying facility. Selwyn's had bought a whole new meaning to a Champagne Breakfast.

Having returned and given a heart rending leaving speech, Selwyn was disappointed that we were one table away from being the last to leave the Restaurant. It was then time for the difficult goodbyes, before we stepped onto terra firma. Would I miss the Erudite? Not particularly. Would I miss Selwyn? Absolutely. As usual in life, it is the people you meet that both make and break your experience.

Is it all about relationships?

ACKNOWLEDGEMENTS

Mrs Funn. My wonderful wife whom I love. Thank you for your support and willingness to be 'referenced' in this ridiculous piece of fiction.

Miss Funn the 1st and 2nd. Thank you for your editing assistance and advice (Miss Funn the 3rd was 'studing').

Miss Libby Whiteside, Graphic Designer. Thank you for interpreting my thoughts and designing the excellent book cover.

The readers of the 'African Volunteering Safari.' Thank you to those of you who encouraged me to write a book. I hope you have enjoyed it and, whether it is a success or not, to quote Mills, "It has been a blast."

Jesus. For giving me life, life to the full.

Printed in Great Britain
by Amazon

41064028R00071